ON THE BORDERS OF REALITY

STRANGE SHORT STORIES

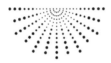

TIMOTHY FOREMAN

Copyright © 2023 by Timothy Foreman

All rights reserved.

No part of this book may be reproduced in any form or by any electronic or mechanical means, including information storage and retrieval systems, without written permission from the author, except for the use of brief quotations in a book review.

INTRODUCTION

This book is full of strange, unique stories. It contains plot twists, monsters, heroes, and other worlds. While all these stories are uniquely different, they all have the same underlying theme—the mystery of human existence.

FOREST DEMON

"Die with memories, not regrets." Those were the words I had tattooed on my upper right arm, etched in front of a globe with a plane flying around it. It was a modification of a similar quote representing a belief I once firmly held. "We regret the actions not taken, not the things we do. We regret the experiences we miss out on rather than the ones we have."

I received the tattoo when I still believed and lived by such words back before the incident. That was one experience I wish I had missed out on, one there is no coming back from. Those events are forever etched on my brain, perhaps even eternally on my soul. Visions and knowledge of horrors I wish I had never learned.

It happened almost a year ago during the summer. My friend Jerry wanted to go on a five-day hiking trip across a foothills trail that runs through the mountains on the western side of the North and South Carolina border.

I had been friends with Jerry for many years. Our shared interests in alternative belief systems and unusual experiences drew us together. We were obsessed with the paranormal and ancient beliefs. He took a particular interest in cults and so-called dangerous religious ideas. Growing up in the bible belt, finding people who shared these interests was difficult, so our bond was strong.

Jerry was also curious about family lineages. According to family legend, his grandfather was part of some mysterious secret society. Jerry's mother said she didn't know if it were the Freemasons, Rosicrucians, or some other nameless order. His grandfather never talked about it. All his mother remembered was that a few times a year his grandfather would leave home late in the evenings and only return in the mornings. Most of the time when he returned, he would fix breakfast, talk and joke with his kids, and then go take a nap after their meal, acting like nothing out of the ordinary happened. However, Jerry's mother remembers a few times when her father was very quiet after coming back. She said he would just stare off into space with something clearly on his mind. But when she asked him what he was thinking of, he would tell her, "Nothing of concern," and disappear into his study. Apparently, he never napped on those days, staying up late into the night.

Jerry didn't have too many memories of his grandfather since he shot himself when Jerry was only five years old.

Jerry and his mother recently visited his aunt over the weekend of his cousin's wedding. His aunt let him rummage through her attic, where she kept some family heirlooms and stuff belonging to her parents. In one box, he found several books belonging to his grandfather. Most were just war stories. But there was one book in particular that caught his attention. He didn't tell me anything about it other than he would bring it on our trip and that I would find it fascinating.

We met up early on a Friday morning at a park that held one of the trailheads for the trek. As usual, his bag was twice the size of mine. He had packed cooking items, a tent, and extra food. I had packed rope, a tarp, a compact hammock, beef jerky, and workout clothes that were good at absorbing sweat. I was faster and had more endurance as a long-distance runner than Jerry, but he was stronger and better built. I was not interested in carrying heavy weights over long distances.

We were climbing a steep slope right away, with the track's elevation rising drastically over a short distance. We were drained by the time we got to the first lookout after three and a half hours. We came up on a granite rock overlooking valleys and mountains of pristine wilderness. The breathtaking view made all the struggle worthwhile. Seeing such a wide expanse without buildings, roads, and people reminded me that society really only takes up a small portion of the world. All its rules and restrictions are not as inescapable as one might believe. All its suppressions, stress, and time obligations that we find so overbearing are ultimately voluntary. Society is not a prison we can't leave, even though that is easily forgotten when you're part of it. For me, being reminded of that makes bearing it much more tolerable.

These Appalachian Mountains aren't as large or magnificent as the Rockies or Alps, but they are much older. It feels like I am connected to something ancient in their wilderness.

After eating lunch, we continued our journey for several hours. When the sun started approaching the horizon, we decided to set up camp in a valley near the river. I tied my hammock between two trees, spread a tarp above it using ropes and stones to anchor it, and then helped Jerry set up his tent.

After we settled down, Jerry reached into his bag and

pulled out the book. It was of a good size and looked old, like it had been through a lot. It was a hardcover that seemed to be bound in human skin. There were dust flecks pressed in its cracks. It was difficult to make out the title due to its age and condition, but I did discern the words "Daemonium Invocticus."

Jerry said he had been reading the book, and it seemed to call upon different legendary spirits. Flipping through the book, I saw many arcane symbols and what looked like scribbles of an old language I did not recognize.

Jerry said it was Latin. He knew a little bit from what he taught himself, but we had a friend going to school for theology and religious studies who helped him translate a couple of the chapters.

Jerry wanted to try an experiment, a ritual to call upon a mountain spirit or demon. I was excited. Neither of us knew about or were overly concerned about the kind of dangers that might be involved in a summoning. We didn't even consider the intentions of such a being. We just wanted to experience the supernatural, to touch something beyond the physical realm.

Of course, I'm not sure how much a part of me truly believed anything would happen. While I firmly believed in the spirit world and that it could overlap with ours under certain circumstances, I was sceptical that anyone could purposely affect it. My own past failed experiences convinced me of it.

There was one time in high school that I did manage to experience the spirit world. I had been trying to astral project (leave my body as a spirit) by using different visualisation and meditation techniques. But none of those techniques seemed to work. One night I was relaxing in a warm bath and prayed to my "spirit guides," which I had read about earlier that day. That night, as I climbed into bed, I leaned on my right hand with my arm straight and suddenly got an overwhelming feeling I was being watched. I could feel a gaze fixed on me from the area in front of my closet. I was too afraid to lay all the way down on my bed. Frozen in place. I had never felt like that before or since. It took tremendous courage to finally move and lay in bed. As soon as I did, the blankets closest to the closet rose quite distinctly as if something had gone under them. After about a minute, I put my hand on the blanket and pushed it down. It went down like nothing was under it. I ran to turn on my light and slept with it on for the next few months. Even now, as an adult, when I am alone at night and think about it too much, I have to leave the light on to sleep.

So perhaps that prayer did invoke the thing in my room that night.

Jerry, using a stone he found by the river, drew a circle in the soft ground a couple of meters from the river. He copied over some symbols from the book onto the ground, drawing triangles inside the circle with corners pointing straight out to make a hexagram.

He told me there was supposed to be a full moon that night, which was one of the reasons he scheduled the trip for this weekend. He placed stones along the circle at each corner of the hexagram. When everything was done, he set his alarm for three in the morning, saying it was the witching hour. We woke up to do the incantation. The moon was partially covered by clouds when we walked to the circle. We stood outside the circle since it was not meant to protect us, as I had previously thought, but to keep the spirit trapped within. Jerry spoke a Latin incantation while holding a symbol out in front of him. He had carved it from a piece of willow wood before their trip. He repeated the incantation three times, and then we waited.

Nothing happened. We waited for around fifteen minutes with no results. It was a massive disappointment as the ritual had invoked intense feelings of anticipation.

Jerry said, "Well, that's it."

I let out a deep sigh, partly from disappointment and partly out of relief. I don't know how I would have reacted if something had actually appeared in the circle. As we made to leave and return to our shelters, I got an intense feeling of being watched. I figured it was my imagination going wild from the failed ritual. However, the feeling persisted and was as strong as I had experienced in my room that night long ago. Then Jerry asked if I had a creepy feeling something was watching us. I answered in the affirmative and asked if I could sleep in the tent with him; he agreed rather quickly.

After we had climbed into our sleeping bags and settled in for the night, I heard a crunching noise outside the tent near my head. It sounded like something was moving out there. Then I heard another in front of the tent. That's when Jerry said, "Yeah, that's not normal." I figured it was an animal, albeit one of a considerable size. I heard something slide against the tent wall near my head again. After a few more minutes of hearing nothing else, I drifted off to sleep.

I woke up with the sun just above the mountains. I pulled on my shirt and got out of the tent to find Jerry already boiling some coffee over the fire.

I started walking around the areas I thought I had heard the noises the previous night, looking to discern some tracks and get a clue of what might have been lurking in our campsite. I saw a group of tracks in the red dirt that was pretty well-defined on the heel. Whatever made them must have had a great deal of mass. A bear perhaps? The tracks seemed to indicate the animal had come through the circle. In fact, a part of the circle seemed pretty scuffed up. But only one part of the circle looked corrupted. Perhaps the animal stepped over the rest of the circle. Another print in the circle seemed headed toward the scuff mark. It was the only one I could see in the circle.

"Looking for tracks?" Jerry asked. "Strange, Isn't it?"

I just told him it must be a bear.

"Think so? You see that one by the river?" he pointed at an incline dipping into the river of soft dirt. I walked over to take a look. It was big and well-defined. In fact, I thought it was bigger than a bear, and it was nothing like the print of a bear. It was shaped like a man's.

About ten hours down the trail, we found a good spot to set up camp for the night. It was a flat clearing surrounded by trees with a river nearby. After setting up, we put on our swimming trunks and headed towards a trail that led to a waterfall. According to the map, the waterfall was about a mile down the trail.

Along the way, we reminisced about old entertainment media we enjoyed as kids, like old movies and video games. There were a few other trekkers present when we arrived at the waterfall. They all looked to be in their early twenties. One of the hikers was a tall, lanky guy with thick, curly brown hair that hung down to about the middle of his neck. There were two girls with him, a young blonde and a brunette. They all looked pretty fit. They stood dead still and were quietly staring off into space as we approached. They seemed to be lost in thought.

"Greetings," we announced as we came upon them. The blonde seemed startled out of her daze and said, "Hello." I asked how long they had been on the trail, and they told me a couple of days.

"How has your journey been so far?" I asked. The guy replied it had been good.

"Ours has been good as well, but it is hard to get a good night's sleep so far away from our comfortable homes. By the way, my name is Tim, and this is my friend Jerry."

The guy replied, saying his name was Ted before introducing the blonde as Caroline and the brunette as Patricia. He then added in a deep and solemn voice, "Yeah, it is hard to sleep out here, especially after earlier this morning."

"What do you mean?" I asked.

"I woke up early to set up a fire, cook biscuits for the girls and me, and brew some coffee. I started to smell a stench like rotten eggs or something. It didn't smell like a skunk. I heard a noise like a deep roar coming from behind me to my left. I jumped up in fright and knocked over some pots and pans that were on a stump; I made quite the ruckus. As soon as I did, I heard a loud crackling that sounded like sticks breaking, or more like small trees. Then I heard an animal running. It must have been huge. I saw a few tall trees through the spaces of other trees falling like they were being pushed over. Whatever it was, it was moving fast. The girls woke up in fright. Patricia was screaming."

The guy's eyes grew wide as he relayed their story, and his face flushed. I could see the fright painted on his face; terror still embedded in him as he recalled the event.

"We were too frightened to go anywhere for a couple of hours," Caroline said. "Ted went and investigated the area the creature seemed to have been at."

Ted continued, saying, "Branches were crushed, trees were pushed over, and some looked like their roots had just been ripped out of the earth. The trees were just overturned, uprooted."

Originally, our plan was to stay on the trail for a week, but we are about a day and a half from civilization, so we're cutting the trip short. We can't travel in the dark, so we will rest here and head up a little further on the trail. We need to find a good spot to stay hidden for the night. Hopefully, we will make it out of here by tomorrow afternoon or evening. I suggest y'all do the same. Get out as soon as you possibly can."

"Perhaps whatever it was, was frightened off by your activity. We will finish the trail," Jerry said.

"Well Godspeed to y'all. Be safe. I would not take a chance of getting a closer look at that thing." With that, they took off. Jerry looked at me.

"What do you make of that? Do you think it could be the same thing that was around our camp last night?"

"It seems plausible," I said. "Let us fill up our water containers. I think we should find a place nearby to set up camp so we can enjoy the waterfall this evening."

We found a good spot about a quarter of a mile from the falls. Jerry set up his tent, and I tied up my hammock and tarp. I put my swim trunks back on, and we went back to the waterfall to cool off and relax. We stayed there until dusk started to set in before going back to camp. Jerry set up a fire to cook a typical backpacking meal.

"You know it was a silent hike today," Jerry said.

"What do you mean?" I asked.

"Didn't you notice? We heard birds and regularly saw snakes cross the trail over the last couple of days. But today, we didn't see or hear any animals."

"Now that you mention it, you're right. We didn't encounter any wildlife today."

"Yes, it is strange…" Jerry said, trailing off in thought.

Just then, we heard a woman scream from further up the trail. We looked at each other, our eyes wide.

"We should go check that out," I said.

"I'm not so sure. We don't have any weapons for defence," Jerry said.

"I have my survival knife. It is better than nothing. Look, if we both go, we might have a greater advantage against whatever it is," I said.

We ran in the general direction of the scream, a little unsure if we would be able to find where it was coming from. We got to a point where we could see a fire up ahead and heard a ruckus coming from there that sounded like a struggle. By the time we came to the spot, the camp was destroyed. Tent fragments were thrown everywhere. Bags were emptied and ripped apart. What kind of creature could just rip a backpack apart? Gear and food were thrown everywhere. There was a dark stain of what looked like blood on the trunk of a tree. The place looked like a crime scene. I saw a shadow move between some trees nearby, a large shadow just outside the firelight's reach before it melded deeper into the woods.

"What the hell happened here?" Jerry asked as if the forest might give an answer.

"This is the camp of those people we ran into earlier, isn't it?" he said.

"I don't know, I guess it could be," I replied.

Jerry shook his head, saying, "No, it definitely is. Look." He pointed up at a tree, his eyes were wide with fright. Before I even looked up at what he was pointing at, fear gripped me as I saw the panic in his eyes. I looked up at the tree and saw Ted's face in the branches, or actually his head and just his head. There was blood staining the tree underneath him.

"Oh, my God! Who or what could do that?" I exclaimed. It looked like his head had been ripped off.

"I suspect the ritual worked. We brought a demon out

into this forest. They were right to try and cut their trip short and get out of here. Unfortunately, they were too late. We need to get our stuff and leave now," Jerry said.

We went back to our camp. It was getting dark. We had flashlights, but I wasn't sure that trying to find our way out of these woods in the dark was the best course of action. We could easily get lost. But the alternative of staying where we were and being a sitting target was not appealing. Moving on was probably our best chance of making it through the night. We had no real way of defending ourselves against such a strong, ruthless beast.

As we approached our camp at a brisk pace, I smelled an awful odour, like a skunk or sulphur mixed with something horrid. A horrible piercing wail came from the direction of our campsite. The scream wasn't entirely human but still distinctly primate. I saw part of Jerry's tent streak through the air above our campsite, followed shortly by a huge stone. The noise came again, and its sheer power made me tremble, striking a terror in me I had never felt before. A terror that came from some deeply ancestral and primitive part of my mind. It disoriented me. We lost all care for our stuff at the campsite and ran away from the noise.

We ran as fast as we could and as far as we could further down the trail. I realized there was no way we could keep this up till we found civilization. We were over a day's hike away. We found a camp clearing by the river with some thick brush beside the clearing. I pointed it out to Jerry, and we went to hide in it. We hid there for a few minutes in complete silence. I thought the beast must not have followed us after not seeing it for a while, but then it stepped out where I could barely see it by the moon's light.

It looked like a big ape-man. In fact, it looked a lot like what people call bigfoot or sasquatch. It was huge, standing at around seven feet tall, with brownish-reddish fur. Its head was oddly conical at the top. The beast was sniffing and looking around with apparent intention and intelligence. It seemed to know we were there but could not figure out where. It let out a piercing roar that curdled our blood. The sound was otherworldly. No creature of this world could ever make such a sound. It finally walked off deep into the forest.

It knew we were there. Perhaps it was taking off to give us a sense of comfort and lure us out of hiding. For what seemed like forever, we did not dare move. Jerry was the first to stir. "I have an idea," he said. "We need to remake the circle with the symbol so we can trap him. We will leave a small part of the circle open until he enters it. Once he is in, we can quickly complete the circle."

"Do you remember how to draw the symbol inside the circle?" I asked.

"Yes," he said.

Jerry did always have a good memory. He found a stick and started drawing in the dirt. As he was doing that, we heard movement in the forest. The beast was running straight for the clearing. Jerry wasn't finished drawing the symbol yet. I looked around for a weapon and saw a stone about the size of my head nearby. I picked it up and threw it with all my strength at the stomping sound coming at us. I was exhausted from the night's flight, but a second dose of adrenalin helped me throw the stone further than I should have been able to under normal circumstances.

The stone merely bounced off the beast. He looked at me and started to come at me. I dodged to the right just before the beast could trample me. It seemed to be slow in changing direction. Jerry said some words in Latin, drawing the beast's attention back toward him. It ran at him, stopped in front of him in the circle, and made to reach out and grab him. I spotted the incomplete section of the circle directly behind the creature. It was just a few inches across. Without time to find a stick, I ran over and used my fingers to shape the rest of the circle in the dirt. The creature's hand stopped just inside the circle before reaching Jerry, who barely stood outside its perimeter.

The beast stared at us. I could see it was angry. It looked at us with hate and bloodlust, but it seemed helpless. Nevertheless, I hardly felt secure with only a drawing in the ground between us and it. I suppose the laws of magic are strange.

"Do you know how to make it disappear again?" I asked Jerry.

"No. I would need the book and that is probably ripped apart along with everything else we left behind."

"What happens to it then? Does it disappear when the sun rises or turn invisible, or will it still be here?" I asked.

"I don't know. But I don't think we should hang around to find out," he said.

"We are still a long way from escaping these woods," I replied.

"Yes, but I can't sleep, can you?"

"No, and we have no bags now, so we can make better timing. Let's go," I said.

We walked for the rest of that night and late into the next day, following the trail out onto a mountain dirt road. We followed that road to a main road and hitchhiked back into town, where we finally called a friend to pick us up.

The incident took place some years ago. Neither of us has been backpacking, hiking, or camping since then. Were we wrong to just leave the demon there where it could possibly terrorize others? Perhaps. I wish I could say we were heroic and took care of it, or at least figured out a way to banish it and returned to the woods to do so. But fear can make a man do shameful things. It can compel him to do things that make him no longer fit to be called a man. Thinking back at the look in the beast's eyes the last time we saw it, I doubt it would give us another chance. I doubt we could survive another encounter with it.

I don't know what happened to the creature, nor do I have any desire to go back and find out. However, in the last few years, there have been mysterious disappearances in the western mountains of North Carolina. Some people even claim to have spotted a bigfoot-like creature in those woods.

PHILOSOPHY CLASS OF THE DEATH EXPERIENCE

Mrs. Hunter

Erica Hunter was a woman who had been inquisitive all her life. She was especially curious about the deeper questions in life. The "unanswerables", as she called them. Questions like, "What is the meaning of life?" and "What are the right and wrong choices in certain complicated moral situations?" Or even questions like, "Who are we?" and "What is reality?" She was also interested in more concrete unanswerables, such as "Are we alone in the universe?" and "What happens to us after we die?"

These questions are what drew her to philosophy. She had known she wanted to delve into it ever since she was in high school, checking out books in her local library on Kant and Neitzche and reading the entries in the encyclopedia of philosophy in the library's reference section. So when she went to college, she decided to major in it.

Unfortunately, there is little one can do with such a

degree to make money. You either write books with some credibility or teach. So she minored in education and started to teach philosophy.

She managed to convince the school board at her high school to add a philosophy program and started teaching there. There was some resistance to the subject at first. Some board members didn't see any practical benefit of teaching philosophy in high school. But Erica had a persuasive way about her. She told them the kids would learn to think for themselves, to think outside the box, and to not just accept what is taught to them without understanding it first. She argued these benefits were why it was important for kids to learn philosophy at an early age. So, North Oak High School got an Intro to Philosophy class.

Erica's mother died of liver issues over that summer, so she started to think a lot about what happens after death. She read books about the afterlife, including the *Tibetan Book of the Dead*, an old book used to guide a soul's journey through the afterlife, and *Life After Life*, an early collection of near-death experiences. She found the similarities between the recounted experiences very interesting, considering that the book was written before the concept of near-death experiences was widely known. She also sought out stories where people described observing what happened around their bodies, or even outside their bodies, with extreme accuracy. She was intrigued by the accounts of people feeling as if they were out of their bodies or observing themselves from a different vantage point.

One thing she liked about teaching philosophy is she could gain new and different ideas on interesting topics from young minds. She decided she would come up with a new assignment this year. She would have her students reflect on the phenomenon of near-death experiences and form their own ideas of what may be going on.

"Class," she announced as she was explaining the course syllabus on the first day back at school, "this week I want you to study the phenomena of near-death experiences. I am specifically referring to the visions people report seeing when they are on the edge of death, in a deep coma, or returned from being declared clinically dead. Tell me about the things that stand out to you and what you think might be going on. Try to come up with ideas that have not been thought of before, something creative. You will write a short paper on the topic and present it in front of the class next Tuesday."

"I have a handout for you that provides a brief overview and some firsthand accounts of people's experiences. Familiarize yourself with it but feel free to look for more sources. The overview discusses the similarities between the experiences, highlighting common themes, such as the tunnel to light, universal love, feeling one with something far beyond the ego, a world of light, meeting with loved ones, and out-of-body experiences. That is your assignment for next week."

Ivan

Ivan was a stereotypical sci-fi nerd. His room was full of *Star Trek* spaceship models and posters of alien movies. He loved sci-fi video games and movies, particularly *The Twilight Zone* for its historical importance of bringing the science fiction genre to the big screen. He also loved comics about superheroes since they were just another version of science fiction.

Ivan and his friends spent their time talking about the

latest movies and what was happening with the X-men and the Avengers in their worlds. Whenever they could all get together for a few hours, they played video games and even *Stars Without Numbers*, a science fiction RPG game similar to *Dungeons and Dragons*.

Ivan was not much of a fan of school, but every once in a while, they would teach something interesting in science about space or technology. Sometimes in history, they would talk about war and knights. But for the most part, school subjects were pretty dull compared to the exciting science fiction worlds he was used to. He supposed much of the real world was equally dull.

When he elected classes for the new semester, he tried to select ones that were easy to get through. His older brother had recommended the Intro to Philosophy class. He took it a previous year and said it was a breeze. They even occasionally discussed interesting science fiction-type topics, such as immortality and time travel. The instructor, Mrs. Hunter, was apparently very interested in that type of stuff. So Ivan thought it would be an easy A and signed up for it.

He was not happy about receiving an assignment on the first day of school and then having to write and present it the next week. He hated public speaking and wondered if this had been a mistake. But he would continue to give it a chance. His brother wouldn't steer him wrong on this, would he? After all, he still had a few weeks to drop the class if he needed to.

That night he read the handout with scepticism. If these accounts were true, there would not be so many people who doubted the afterlife, and most people do. He wondered why not everyone who recovered from clinical death had these experiences. This is what gave him his idea.

In class that next Tuesday, Ivan was the first to be called up to the front. His hands were sweaty, and he was nervous.

He did not know how Mrs. Hunter would react to what he wrote as it was quite unorthodox. But she did say she wanted creative explanations.

"What stood out to me about these experiences is that not everyone goes through them or reports experiencing them when they come back from clinical death. So, perhaps only some people have a soul." As he said soul, he mimed air quotation marks with his hands, indicating he thought this was not the best term to use. "Perhaps there is an alien race far more technologically advanced and more evolved than us that came to Earth in incorporeal forms to live human lives. Maybe they live several. Perhaps mimicking our life and immersing in our cultures is their way of studying faraway alien species. Perhaps they live longer than us. Their incorporeal forms could be temporary due to some technology. Or maybe it is their true form, and they use it to travel the universe, learning about different alien cultures by living the lives of that species. Perhaps even their planet is incorporeal, completely invisible and much closer to us than we realize."

"They forget who they are because they have to start from scratch when they're born as another species to truly know what it is like to be them. They must learn the species' languages, how they utilize their senses, and their way of thinking without the influence of former memories and knowledge getting in the way. Perhaps their minds are so advanced that other species' brains, such as ours, can't handle it, so it is an automatic process for them to forget who they are while living as a different species."

He looked at Mrs. Hunter. She was staring at him. He was expecting a polite form of "What the hell was that?" Instead, she smiled and said, "That was very good. I liked that. You are thinking. Very creative, Ivan. You may sit down"

As Ivan walked back to his seat, he thought maybe this wasn't a mistake after all.

Kathy

Kathy always had goals. She wasn't happy unless she was working on something to better herself. She studied Arabic from an early age and was already considered fluent. She played the violin, was part of the fencing club, took belly dancing classes downtown, and was in the chess club. She liked to do things that made her stand out. Things that few other people were doing.

Part of her motivation came from trying to live up to her parents' success. Her father was a cardiologist, and her mother was a psychiatrist. She planned to eventually go into the medical field and follow in their footsteps. They had high expectations of her and expected her to keep up good grades as well as maintain extracurricular activities. Sometimes she was stressed out and tired, but she always pushed through, motivated to be the best that she could be.

A boy named Justin, whom she met in class, introduced her to philosophy. He told her about Aristotle, Seneca, and stoicism. She found it very interesting. Of course, it helped that she found the boy interesting too. She always focused on her goals and they took priority in her life. She wasn't planning on even thinking about relationships until she had finished medical school, but teenagers are bound to have crushes no matter how much they resist.

She signed up for the Intro to Philosophy class to learn more about it. The assignment given on the first day was interesting. She never gave much thought to the afterlife. Her parents were atheists, and she believed there was nothing after death. Her dad would say there was comfort in Albert

Einstein's theory of time. In fact, Albert Einstein had written a letter about it to comfort the wife of a friend who had recently passed away. It basically said that time is an illusion and that the past, present, and future happened simultaneously, so the person was never truly gone. At least, that was the way Kathy understood it.

She also read some studies on extrasensory perception—the overall term for telepathy, clairvoyance, and precognition. She found that some studies seemed to support it while others didn't. She knew that premonitions were reported by people from all cultures through the ages. Her cousin, who she trusted, claimed to have had a dream of a wreck the night before it happened. The wreck happened the same way with the same red Buick and at the same crossroads as in the dream. Of course, sceptics would chalk it up to crossroads being places where wrecks are more likely to occur. They would blame it all on false memory and chance, or a combination of them. After all, how many times do people dream of wrecks and nothing happens? Although she had never heard of her cousin dreaming about wrecks before.

She believed that if ESP did exist, it could all be precognition. After all, it was a simplified theory that used Occam's razor. It also explains why no physical signal has been detected in association with telepathy and clairvoyance. Besides, precognition can surely be mistaken for both of them. Francis Bacon, the founder of the scientific method, believed in it. Tachyons, particles that travel faster than the speed of light and send information back in time, could exist. They show up in many string theories. Even many people in the government's Stargate program came to believe someone's future mental state could send information back to someone's past mental state.

Mrs. Hunter wanted a unique perspective, so she would give her utmost to do just that. As her turn came to present her project, she walked up to the front of the class with confidence. She never minded presenting her work. She always put in extra effort to make it the best she could. It helped that this project was easy and interesting.

"What I found the most interesting about near-death experiences is the reported sense of being outside of time, or experiencing 'eternity' as some people referred to it," she said. "It seems they generally experience this when they go into the light. Before this, many experienced what is referred to as a life review, where they relive their whole lives in extreme detail over a short period. Along with this, they also realize how they affected everyone else in their lives. This implies they are experiencing time differently than we do in life. When they experience being outside of time, they also experience being one with something greater than their ego. Some people call it divinity, some say it's all life, while others say it's the whole universe or everything. Perhaps this comes from their difficulty in explaining it, or maybe they are unsure about what the source of that feeling of oneness is."

"What if what they are experiencing is the oneness of the past, present, and future of their lives? They have become one with time or the timespan of their lives. Maybe during life, our consciousness can only experience each moment in succession. On an atomic scale, physicists cannot tell the difference between time running one way or the other. They can't tell if it's running backwards or forwards. Albert Einstein said that time was an illusion, albeit a stubborn one. What if some part of our brain creates this illusion of linear time so we can experience life as a series of moments and experiences? Maybe in the process of dying, that part of the brain dies, so the illusion disappears and people experience time—or at least their life—as it truly is. One giant moment, an instant happening all at once that has always existed somewhere in the stream of time. Perhaps this is how people come back with knowledge they shouldn't have. They pull it from the information they obtain in the future when they are in a state where all of time is one moment. They see themselves from a fourth dimension perspective, and the fourth dimension is a dimension of time."

Mrs. Hunter looked at her and asked, "If all of time, including the future, has already happened, what does that say about free will?"

"I think you're looking at it from a present-moment point of view," Kathy told her. "It is hard not to because that is how we experience life. The past has already happened, but that doesn't mean that you didn't have free will in those moments. If you think of time as a spatial landscape, knowledge or vision of the future would just be like seeing or knowing what is going on a few miles away. It doesn't mean those events are affected or determined. We know from Einstein's theory of relativity that time is not what our common sense would dictate. Why should it be? Our brains didn't evolve to solve the mysteries of the universe, they just gave us a survival advantage. It does go against common sense, but if common sense was always right, there would be no need for science." she exclaimed.

"Well, we will talk about free will and time in a future lecture," Mrs. Hunter said. "Very good, Kathy. You may sit down."

The fact that her presentation lead to a big topic in philosophy motivated Kathy to further improve her grade. She sat down with a smile, satisfied that she had made her classmates think. Actually, it was more of a smirk. The kind one might wear when feeling superior to one's peers.

Trevor

Trevor came from a poor family. He lived on the side of town that most people wanted to forget. In fact, the city and county governments did seem to forget his area. There were potholes scattered on the roads in the neighbourhood that made for a rough ride. The fanciest cars driving through the area were police cars and the occasional DSS worker. Most people did their best to avoid driving through the area and go the long way around instead.

Some houses had been abandoned by people for as far back as Trevor could remember. They were now mostly occupied by overgrown plants and vines crawling up the outside walls. He was sure that many critters had moved into those. There was an old abandoned mill nearby where most of the townspeople had worked back in the day. Now the town was a ghost, a shadow, of its former self.

Trevor lived with his dad. His mom left his dad when he was three, and neither of them has seen her since. Trevor's father drank a lot. He was never sure if his dad started drinking because his mother left or if she left because of his drinking. He couldn't remember that far back, and he learned that his mother was a topic best to avoid around his father. When his father gets angry, he starts yelling and cussing and will sometimes even get rough with Trevor. Of course, that only happened when he was drinking, but he was always drinking.

His father could barely keep a job because of alcohol, and when he did, it was usually temporary. Trevor couldn't remember the last year he got to eat a real Thanksgiving meal. Last year, his Thanksgiving meal was a bologna sandwich. Thankfully, they usually had food since his father stockpiled canned food whenever possible. Although it mostly consisted of bread, peanut butter and jelly, or bologna.

Meth was a big problem in his neighbourhood. People were up all night in the streets, and the commotion made it difficult to sleep many nights. He regularly heard fights break out not far from his room. One time they woke up with no power because people had stolen wires to sell as scrap metal.

So Trevor escaped his world into horror books that he checked out at the local library. He loved Stephen King and H.P. Lovecraft. Their stories seemed to show a darker side of the world than most other stories. That was how Trevor saw the world too. He saw its dark side.

Trevor didn't really have friends at school, so he kept to himself with his head tucked down. He stuck to his books. He didn't trust people anyway and figured friends would just take advantage of him at the first opportunity. That's what his father always told him too. He had brought a friend home once, and his dad kicked him out, saying he didn't want any extra damn kids in the house; one was more than enough.

Trevor often had a hard time focusing at school. So, when he had heard that Intro to Philosophy was a pretty easy class, he figured he wouldn't have to focus on it too much. The assignment on the first day of class didn't seem like it would be too difficult. He just had to give an opinion on some people hallucinating as they died. He thought it sounded like a fun trip.

After reading about near-death experiences and all the pleasant visions people had of the afterlife and God, he got a bit angry. He didn't believe in that stuff because it sounded too good to be true. The idea of still existing after death was pushing it, but for it to be such a beautiful existence was ludicrous. The world was dark. He knew that was the truth. Everything that contradicted that was just wishful thinking.

If a god did exist, it was a dark god, an evil god. He could believe that. He could always tell how likely something was to be true by how pessimistic it was.

When his turn came to present his project, Trevor walked up to the front of the class with his head down, looking at the floor and avoiding any eye contact with the rest of the students. Knots were tying in his stomach. He hated this part. He stood in front of the room, feeling sweaty. He knew he probably stunk like he sometimes did.

"What I found interesting about these events was the light they kept mentioning. It was full of love, peace, joy, and bliss. People reported these feelings were enhanced to a degree that we cannot fathom here on Earth. I find it interesting that this great cosmic force conveniently presents all the things that people love the most. Exactly what they love the most." Trevor said.

"It reminds me of those lights people keep outside on their porches. The ones that kill bugs by shocking them. In the dark, the bugs are drawn to the light. These people were in the dark, both figuratively and literally. They were confused because they had just died and now found themselves before an alluring light at the end of a dark tunnel or space. They are immediately drawn straight to this light that only projects the feelings and emotions people are typically drawn to. What if that's the whole point? After entering the light, people described a sense of feeling at one with everything. It sounds like their ego, their self, their individuality was being eaten away. I imagine if that process had been completed, they wouldn't have returned. Maybe this thing eats souls or people's life forces or whatever. It tricks people with an alluring light and warm emotions so it can devour what is left of them."

"So this is a deceit, a devil in disguise perhaps," Mrs. Hunter said. "We will be talking about what the truth is in another lecture. It certainly can be hard, if not impossible, to tell. That was quite a doom and gloom view you got from something so positive. Interesting. You may take a seat."

Trevor went back to his seat, his eyes glued to the floor the whole time. He felt relieved that the presentation was over. It felt like a weight had been lifted off his shoulders. He sat down and slumped in the seat.

∽

Escape

Mrs. Hunter was proud of how the new assignment had gone. She found it amazing how many different ways one mysterious phenomenon could be viewed and interpreted. She thought about some of the ideas her students had presented in class. Many had brought up things that could be tied into future lectures.

What she found most interesting was what these ideas said about her students, their life experiences, and their personalities. Each idea hinted at something deep inside them. One of her students, Kathy, likes to play the role of the intellectual. She wanted people to see that about her, so she tried to mention advanced science principles in her presentation. Another student, Trevor, shared a perspective that betrayed his untrusting nature. And Ivan seemed curious about life in outer space. Perhaps he was interested in escaping to the stars.

Perhaps they were all interested in escaping their present lives. That's human nature, she supposed. Ever since people gathered around a fire at night, they would tell stories. They would tell myths of other worlds and other beings. Then people started to write stories down so people could read and escape into them on their own. Where psychedelics were used for ages in certain cultures, people now used streaming and games to escape the mundaneness of their physical existence. Yes, she supposed there would always be people desiring to escape this life.

A STRANGE HAUNTING

Todd hated coming home from school. While most kids couldn't wait for school to end, he couldn't wait for it to begin. School was an escape for him. It was an escape from the horrors at home. It wasn't video games, cartoons, and bikes that Todd had waiting for him. It was a real-life monster, his father.

Todd's father, Jim, was an officer of the law for Henderson County and was well-respected among his peers. He was known for having his partner's back and was great at bringing in the baddies. The "lowlives", as Jim would call them, weren't too fond of him. Of course, to Todd's father, "lowlives" weren't just petty criminals but also anyone who struggled to make ends meet. People around the mill hill who lived in conditions he didn't consider up to his standards were lowlives to Jim. He seemed to look at them like criminals no matter their records. When he talked about those people, he always called them trash and clearly considered himself better than them.

Todd's mother died when he was a baby, so he didn't remember her. It was just Todd and Jim at home with the occasional girlfriend that would stay for a little while until they got tired of Jim's "you are here to serve me" attitude. To Todd, Jim was like a monster. When he was home, Jim got a sadistic kick from throwing his power around and being able to do whatever he wanted to Todd. Jim would throw things in front of Todd and make him clean them up. He once found a beetle in the house and made Todd eat it. He would make him eat food directly off the floor as punishment for talking back. Jim sometimes made him sleep in a closet that was so small Todd had to contract into a fetal position to fit inside. He forced Todd to fill a bathtub with cold water, throw in a bag of ice, and make him sit in it. There seemed no end to his father's sadistic imagination.

Sometimes Jim would beat Todd in the butt and upper legs for doing something as trivial as leaving something out of place. When Jim got his belt ready, he would say, "This is going to hurt you more than it does me," and then laugh at his stupid joke. But it never really seemed to hurt Jim at all. In fact, he took great pleasure in it. He always wore this cocky smirk as he whupped Todd until his butt turned red. After that, Jim would do things in the bedroom to Todd, to his innocence, that no child should be able to understand, let alone experience.

His father warned him if he tried to run away, he would cut off his legs and lock him in the basement. He would keep him there and tell everyone Todd had run away. No one would find him. He told Todd not to tell anyone about the punishments, saying no one would believe or trust him about anything anymore. Todd believed this. After all, his father was a cop. He was a police lieutenant and close with all the cops in Henderson County, including the towns' chiefs and the sheriff.

They had moved into their current home about a year ago when Jim got promoted to lieutenant. It was an old house up in the mountains that had been around since the 20s. There were woods around the house for miles and no neighbours in sight. Todd liked to go out in the woods to avoid his dad whenever he got the chance. He found interesting things in those woods, mainly arrowheads. There was also a big Indian mound about a quarter of a mile from the house. Local legend had it that the area had been considered sacred to Native American tribes for a long time. Near the mound was a big granite stone with a bunch of markings on it. People debated whether these markings were random, natural, or the writings of ancient people. Some said that the writings were from a people who predated the Cherokee tribe that had settled in the area. This was consistent with a Native American legend stating that the stones were there when their people arrived.

The house itself also had a history. The first owners were a family of four. The husband had owned a successful general store in town. The wife stayed at home and took care of their two little girls. One was two, and the other was four. One day, the wife started talking about hearing the devil and believed he was trying to corrupt her children. She had them baptized and blessed. She also started hanging crosses all over the house. About a week after this, the husband came home and found the children drowned in the tub. He lost it and shot his wife and then himself.

The next people to own the house seemed normal, and nothing eventful was known to have happened to them. The ones after them, however, also reported the house was haunted. They were a family with three kids; two boys of six and eight, and a girl of twelve. They said things were inexplicably thrown around the house, and they saw apparitions. However, these events only lasted a little over a year. Two more families lived in the house before Todd and his father moved in. Both of which had nothing unusual to report. In fact, when people asked the last family, they denied anything unusual ever occurring while living there.

Todd and Jim never experienced anything strange during their first year in the house either. Then Todd started hearing footsteps running down the hallway at night. A couple of times, he heard what sounded like a child crying downstairs while he tried to sleep. His father heard the footsteps as well and believed it was Todd. When Todd denied it, his father accused him of lying and made him eat chicken drenched in ghost pepper hot sauce until he puked. Then he made him tiptoe on a piece of wood while balancing a book on his head. He had to do this for fifteen straight minutes, or he would receive a brutal whupping and a night in the closet.

Then things started to move around the house. At first, it started with things not being where anyone had left them, such as Jim's socks in the fridge and milk out on the porch. More things kept showing up in odd places. Of course, Jim assumed Todd was playing pranks and severely punished him for his annoying sense of humor, especially for the ruined milk. Todd had begun to suspect Jim was doing these things in order to justify dishing out more of his artistic torments. After all, Todd had been extremely careful not to make any mistakes. He even spent more time hanging out in the woods to stay out of his father's way.

Todd had strange nightmares ever since they moved into the house. He dreamed of demons trying to possess him and aliens kidnapping him. In one particular dream, he found a cave near the house. When he walked inside, he found it was so dark he couldn't see his hand in front of his face. He could hear a dripping noise. Then a fire blazed out of nowhere, and he saw the cave floor was littered with the bodies of Native Americans covered in blood. They were dead, but still wore expressions of terror fixed on their faces. A large, dark figure steps out of the darkness. At the edge of the firelights' reach,

Todd could just barely make out a humanoid figure that was too large to be human. Fear engulfed him, and he woke up with a start.

Things in the house got worse. Todd saw stuff begin to move around the house of their own accord. He saw spices thrown out of cabinets, and his bedroom door kept opening and closing all by itself. The situation escalated when things started launching themselves at his father from Todd's direction. He saw a shoe lift off the floor near him and fly across the room over his father's shoulder while his father faced the other way watching TV. Jim was pissed, believing Todd had thrown the shoe at him. He made Todd sleep outside with only a blanket that night. Another time, the lamp beside where Todd was sitting lifted high off the table and fell with a crash that broke the bulb and tore the shade. His father believed he had thrown it on purpose. So Jim built a fire, feeding the flames with Todd's shirts and his bicycle.

Todd realized the house was haunted long before Jim did. To Todd, it seemed the spirit didn't care much for him. It appeared to take the same sadistic pleasure in torturing him as his father did. One night, Todd woke up and couldn't move. He had never experienced sleep paralysis before. His fear increased as he heard an animalistic clicking noise to his right. He strained his eyes as much as possible to see what it was, but he could not turn his head. He saw a shadowy creature that looked furry, almost like a dog-human-type creature. He felt the creature run its finger, or claw, up his leg. Panic gripped him, and he tried with all his might to move a finger, toe, or anything. Finally, the power of movement returned to him, and he bolted upright only to see nothing there.

Another night, as he was falling asleep, he heard a male voice as clear as any other say, "You're mine." He jumped up, looked out his door, and saw nothing down the hall.

One day, Todd's father was in the kitchen when things went crazy. Several of the cupboard doors started opening and closing by themselves. Pots and pans flew out of the cabinets. Dishes crashed to the floor. Todd was also in the kitchen, so Jim tried to find some evidence of trickery, like string or anything that could explain what had just happened. During these futile efforts, they heard an extremely loud noise upstairs, like a bunch of furniture crashing together. This happened while Todd was still in his sight. Jim ran upstairs to search his and Todd's rooms as well as the bathroom. He found nothing strange. With that kind of noise, it seemed impossible that nothing had happened. After that, he was quiet. Lost in thought, he didn't say anything to Todd for the rest of the night. Eventually, Jim tried to navigate his thoughts with the aid of whiskey shots.

He didn't say a word to Todd over the next couple of days. He didn't try to torment him either. Todd began to wonder whether the spirit had a change of heart and was trying to help him. The noise came again one night later that week while they were both downstairs. This time when they went to check on the noise, Todd's bed and dresser were thrown over, and his clothes and linen were strewn everywhere. Jim told Todd to pick it up but didn't say much else.

The next morning Jim said the devil had come into their house and blamed Todd for bringing him there. He said the devil seemed to follow Todd because he never experienced anything when Todd wasn't around. This was true. Jim now kept seeing lights go on and off and doors opening and slamming, but only when Todd was in the house. If it wasn't for the night of the kitchen incident and the noise in Todd's bedroom, he would still be convinced Todd was behind it all.

Todd heard another voice while climbing into bed one night. This time it was a quiet voice that sounded like a child's. It was difficult to make out what it said at first, but it repeated itself more clearly, saying, "Are you ok? What's wrong?"

"Who's there?" Todd asked.

"Something is wrong with Mommy," the voice said. It sounded like the voice was coming from his left, just a few inches from his face. What's more, the soft voice seemed to echo in his thoughts. While he was sure it was not part of his thoughts, Todd struggled to tell if it was coming from inside his head or from an external source. He certainly didn't seem to see anything around him.

"I don't know your mom. Who is she?" Todd said.

"Mommy is acting funny," the voice said. "She's playing make-believe again, talking to imaginary friends."

By now, the voice was much clearer, and Todd was certain it came from somewhere in the room, some invisible spot in space. It was also quite clearly the voice of a little girl.

"It's so cold and wet down here," the girl's voice said. "But we have to get rid of THE DEMONS."

With the last words, the voice suddenly became much louder, deeper, and demonic. It made Todd jump with fright, and he ran downstairs into the kitchen and turned on the lights. After a few hours of calming down, he went back to his room and slept in his closet. It had begun to feel safe in there after so many nights of sleeping in there as punishment. The walls embraced, protected him, and he slept soundly.

The next night he tried sleeping in his bed again. Something woke him in the middle of the night. He wasn't sure what at first, but then he heard the little girl's voice calling his name again.

"What do you want?" Todd managed to get out in a shaky voice.

"Will you play with me?" replied the voice. "Mommy and

Daddy can't because they have holes in their heads. And my sister is no fun."

"I have to sleep," Todd said. "I don't want to play. I want you to leave me alone." He said.

"We can't leave you alone, Todd. He won't let us."

"Who won't let you?"

"The devil. He is here, and he has come for you, Todd. You brought him here. He torments us and won't go away because he wants you. I try not to draw his attention, but sometimes he finds me anyway. Shh, do you hear that?"

It sounded like footsteps running up the stairs and down the hall. They stopped just outside Todd's bedroom door. Todd could see shadow movements through the bottom crack of the door.

"He's here!" the voice shrieked.

The bedroom door flew open, and a dark shadow stood in the doorway. It grew taller and taller until the shadow started covering the ceiling.

To his alarm, Todd woke up the next morning unsure of what had happened after he saw the shadow. Was it a dream? It had seemed too real to be a dream. He couldn't be sure. That evening, Todd and Jim watched an ashtray move through the air and tables slide over the floor. His father started muttering about the devil again, saying Todd needed to be purified somehow. Jim went to bed after this.

For the third night, Todd woke to the sound of the voice calling his name. It said, "Your father sounds like my mother in wanting to purify you. She purified us by baptizing our bodies and spirits in water. Perhaps that's what your father should do for you. Then you can play with us."

"Are you one of the girls who was drowned in the bathtub by their mother long ago?" Todd asked.

"People said our mother did it. But it was the angels.

Bright people came and purified us from the demons. Maybe they can help you with the devil."

"So you are a ghost? Or a dream? I can't be sure. It doesn't feel like a dream, but how will I know when I wake up tomorrow?"

"I can tell you a secret or two that you don't know. In your dad's top left drawer is a bag of cocaine. No one knows about it. He has a reputation to uphold. Also, you should ask him why your mother had so much insulin. Then you will see this is *no dream.*"

The voice changed again with its last words, sounding like a demonic whisper. Todd faded off with the voice's last words and woke up late the next morning. It was ten in the morning on a Saturday. His dad had already left for work. Todd made to head downstairs but stopped in the hall and looked over at his father's room, thinking about what the voice had said. He went into his father's room and opened the top left drawer of the dresser. He sifted through a pile of underwear until he felt a plastic baggy. His eyes shot wide as he pulled it out. There was a white powder in the bag.

He had never seen cocaine before but it was consistent with where the voice had said it would be. Of course, the spirit could have conjured it. But would the spirit need to plant it? Surely it knew where everything was in the house. Todd knew precognitive dreams happened to some people. Could it be that? Was the spirit getting into his head and causing dreams or hallucinations?

When Todd's father got home that night, he could tell Jim was in a bad mood. He had no idea why though. His father never told him about his day. Todd figured he should steer clear, but his curiosity got the best of him. He had to ask exactly what the voice had told him to ask.

"Dad, why did mom have so much insulin that last night?"

Jim stopped, his eyes narrowed, and he slowly turned his head toward Todd.

"What did you say? Your mother died of low blood sugar. She refused to eat because she was depressed, thanks to you. Where did you get this insulin idea?" he yelled. Todd knew he had struck a nerve and could tell there was more to it.

"I-I-I just thought…I just heard," Todd said.

"Heard from where?" he yelled.

"I had a dream is all," Todd said. He didn't want to tell his father about the voice and encourage his devil theory. But Jim wasn't fooled.

"A dream? The devil is giving you dreams now? I am going to rid this house of the devil even if it means I have to get rid of you too."

Jim went to his room and took his revolver out of the closet. He brought it downstairs, put a bullet in the cylinder, spun it quickly, and closed it. Todd was scared and thought his short life was about to end. Jim wiped the revolver with a paper towel and made Todd take it.

"We'll let God decide if we need to get rid of you. We are going to play a game. It's called Russian roulette. There is a bullet in that cylinder. Do not look at it. You're going to put it to your head and pull the trigger," he said, looming over Todd. "You've got a five out of six chance that you will be fine."

As scared as Todd was, it was ingrained in him to obey his father unquestioningly for fear of what he might do. He closed his eyes and tensed his finger on the trigger. He thought about how he would never know what it was like to be an adult or have a wife and family of his own. On the positive side, he thought he wouldn't have to fear his father's wrath anymore. Maybe he could play with that girl on the other side. He squeezed the trigger and heard a "click". Nothing else happened.

Todd breathed out a sigh of relief. His father's face was flat and expressionless.

"Damn," Jim said emotionlessly. He took the gun from Todd, opened the cylinder, and then looked back at Todd with a confused expression.

"Maybe God or the devil does have your back. You pulled the trigger on the bullet. It just didn't go off." He returned to his room to put the gun away and didn't come back out that night.

The next day, Todd went into the woods. This time he didn't just go out to avoid his dad but tried to get away from the house as well. He liked going to the area with the mysterious markings on the stone. The markings were on a stone among other giant granite menhirs painted with stripes of quartz veins. The menhirs almost made a complete circle except for a gap that made an easy path into the centre. The circle wasn't far from the house. You would have been able to see the house if it weren't for the trees in the way.

There were no trees in the centre of these stones. Not even grass or shrubs managed to grow there. It was just bare ground. However, Todd had seen mushrooms growing there a few mornings before. He climbed up and sat on a stone that raised high enough to see the creek at the bottom of the hill. It was the spot he came to think.

A voice behind him called, "Howdy. How do you do?"

Todd looked in the direction of the voice and was relieved to see it wasn't a disembodied voice this time. A man stood behind him wearing a polo shirt and a brimmed hat. He had a dark complexion and looked to be in his thirties or forties.

"Hello," Todd said.

"You live in the old house on the hill over there, don't you?" the man asked. Todd replied in the affirmative.

"I like to come out here; never know what I might find. I like to search for arrowheads and stuff. I hope you don't mind me looking," the man said. Todd said he didn't care.

"Say, have you had any strange experiences in that house?" the man asked.

"What do you mean?" Todd asked.

"I think you would know what I mean if you experienced anything. That house, this place, it is a strange place. Some might say a magical place. It's a crossroads where the spirit world and physical world meet." The man could see the curiosity on Todd's face. "My name is Chris, by the way."

"I'm Todd."

"Well, Todd, you like it here at these stones?"

"I come here often to clear my head," Todd said. "And yes, strange things may have happened in my house." Todd thought having someone to talk to about it might be nice. He had never seen this man before. Could he be the spirit in disguise? Could the spirit leave the house?

"I live in the next house over. It's a bit of a walk, but I have something I'd like to show you," Chris said.

Todd never really got the stranger danger talk while growing up. His dad probably wouldn't discourage him from doing so anyway. So Todd didn't have any worries about talking to strangers. After all, no stranger could be much worse than his dad. "Alright," Todd said.

As they walked, Todd told Chris about the strange things he witnessed in the house. Chris said his family had been at the house they were living in for almost a century. His family had deep roots in this area. His grandmother had been full-blooded Cherokee, so his ancestry was tied to some of the first people on this land.

As they approached the house, Todd could see it was old.

It was a small, one-floor house. The paint was peeling and the exterior walls were weathered. The yard was full of empty plant pots, and there were pieces of wood—nailed together for unknown reasons—half buried in the dirt. Chunks of rusted metal and machinery were all scattered about. As they walked through the graveyard of abandoned hobbies and failed projects, Todd got a sense of deep sadness.

Inside the house, Todd saw a display of arrowheads on the living room wall. Dream catchers were hanging on either side of the display. A beaded curtain separated the kitchen from the living room. Chris pointed at an old rocker in the corner of the room.

"That thing will rock by itself at night sometimes. My mother said she saw my grandmother in it a few times after she had died. She would disappear after a few minutes. Both of us have seen an Indian chief walking in the woods around the house on numerous nights."

"We have even seen lights in the sky. Legend has it that the lights are lamps from the spirits trying to find their way from this world into the next. Just the other day, I was out around those stones and saw the lights in the sky again. I followed them and saw them floating over your house. They were white at first but soon turned to orange and then a deep red. They floated about for a while and then just disappeared into thin air. Like my grandmother's ghost, I suppose."

He went to his room and pulled out an object from his closet. It was a figurine of a human-looking thing with big eyes and a serpent wrapped around its waist and neck. The serpent's head rested on top of the human's head.

"This was my grandmother's. She said she found it out in the woods when she explored it as a child. She said it was buried in the ground at the centre of those stones you were sitting on. What do you think of the writing on the stones?"

he asked Todd. Todd said he wasn't sure what to make of them.

"Cherokee legend has it that they were made by a people who came before them. When they arrived, the Indian mound was already there, as were the markings on the stone. They considered the stones sacred. Nothing could grow in the circle. They believed it could heal all kinds of ailments," he told Todd.

"They believed some sort of magic had been left here by gods from the sky. Have you heard the ancient astronaut theory?" he asked Todd. Todd shook his head.

"It's the idea that aliens from outer space visited us in the ancient past, and that's where our legends and stories of gods and supernatural events come from. I think those stones are some kind of ancient technology that aliens may have left here a long time ago."

"That's a strange belief," Todd remarked.

"Yes, it is, but the events that happen around here are strange. I've studied reports of ghosts and poltergeists and the like. It seems that poltergeists lie when they tell people what they are, and they will often change their story. Sometimes they say they are a certain person's spirit, then they call themselves the devil, only to turn around and say they are a different person's spirit. I also found they will sometimes obey orders. Like if a person tells it to stop turning the lights on and off, it might stop at that moment. There are even reports of people getting them to move certain items in particular ways."

"People who have studied these reports discovered that these poltergeists seemed to get stronger with time and around intense emotions. So the more fear and hate they can create, the stronger they get. This is probably why they try to haunt people. But I am not sure how smart they are. They do seem to know things, but I think they may just be imprints on a psychic field. I think there is energy all around us that reacts to our thoughts, or maybe it might exist in a different dimension. The stronger our thoughts, such as during states of high emotion, the more the energy reacts to them. And the greater the reaction, the longer the imprint lasts on the energy. These stones somehow amplify or gather that energy. They may even draw our world closer to a world filled with that psychic energy."

"I think that's where bigfoot comes from. Maybe some ancient human species, like the Neanderthals, left impressions on that energy in similarly charged areas that may exist around the world."

"That is a wild theory," Todd said. "You said that the energy reacts to thoughts, especially during high emotion, right? But I don't think people think much at all when they're filled with fear or anger. They just react." Todd said.

"No, there is a thought or two during rage and panic. In fact, they are strong enough to drown out weaker thoughts, like those of cool, calm logic." Chris said.

Todd thought about the voice in his room. Did those girls' fear of being drowned in the bathtub imprint on this energy, thus giving it an identity? Were there multiple identities in this energy? He thought about how the voice said the devil was there because of him. It said that right after his father had said it. Perhaps it used the idea as an identity or to create more fear and self-loathing in Todd.

"I have to go," Todd said. "It was nice meeting you."

"Likewise," said Chris. "Let me know if anything else happens at that house, ok?"

"Sure," Todd said.

The whole conversation was strange to Todd. But if his ideas were accurate, he wondered if he could use them.

That night Todd woke up to the voice calling his name again. "You're alive," the voice said. "I am glad."

"Are you referring to the gun incident last night?" asked Todd.

"Yes," the voice said.

"Was it you that stopped it from going off?" Todd asked.

"I like you, Todd. I don't want anything bad to happen to you. That's why I try not to let the devil know where you are."

Todd wasn't sure if the ghost was just taking credit or if it really had protected him. He thought he would use it in case it was like Chris said with thoughts.

"We are friends; you would protect me?" Todd asked in a way that was almost more a statement than a question.

"Of course," replied the voice. "Thank you, I am very tired and have school tomorrow. I am going to sleep now." All was quiet after that, and Todd went to sleep.

That evening, Jim was sitting in the lounge watching television. Todd was busy boiling hotdogs on the stove and heating up some canned chilli. Jim put the remote control on the table beside his chair, but it fell straight to the floor. He was sure he set it near the centre of the table. He's never dropped the remote there before, not even when he's had a couple of beers.

Todd saw the kitchen door open by itself. Then, the hallway light switched itself on. The television went off suddenly, right in the middle of a new episode of Jim's favourite show, *Law and Order*. Todd saw his father clench his fist and narrow his eyes. The silence broke when the kitchen drawers slammed open and forks, spoons, butter knives, and cooking utensils flew everywhere. The house started to go crazy. All the doors were opening and closing, and the electronics switched off and on repeatedly.

Jim shot up from his chair. "That is it! I am tired of this shit!" he yelled in a rage. "You brought the devil into this house, and it is going to end now!"

Jim walked through the living room and into the kitchen. He grabbed the pot of boiling hot dogs on the stove and lifted it up, making ready to swing the it at Todd. But as he swung the pot, he fell backwards. It looked like he had been pushed. The boiling water poured all over his face, and he screamed in agony at the top of his lungs.

Todd heard a voice in his left ear telling him to run. He ran upstairs through the hall and into his room. The door shut itself behind him. Jim's screaming died down and he stomped up the stairs after Todd. He grabbed the door, trying to yank it open. The door would not budge. There was no lock on the door.

"I will kill you just like I did your mother," Jim yelled. "The bitch couldn't keep her mouth shut around other men. You probably ain't even my son, you little asshole! You're an unholy birth. That's why the devil protects you!"

Jim went to his closet and grabbed his shotgun. Todd heard the voice tell him to stand away from the door. Jim shot the gun at the doorknob, punching a hole in the door. He still couldn't get the door to budge. He reloaded the shotgun. As Jim tried to aim the shotgun through the door at him, Todd saw the shotgun turn upward. The gun inched ever higher, and Todd saw a scared look creasing his father's face. He was trying to resist the gun from turning upward. The shotgun's barrel ended underneath Jim's chin. There was a loud BOOM! The sound was deafening. Bits and pieces of Jim's head scattered all over the walls and floor of the hallway outside of Todd's room. Jim's body dropped to the floor.

TIMOTHY FOREMAN

~

When police and emergency personnel came to the house, they took Todd to a foster home. The police found the house in a total mess and couldn't believe Todd had been living in such conditions. The official report of the events was an attempted murder and successful suicide. It seemed pretty clear-cut from the scene the house was left in.

Todd was upset; it was his father, after all. But he couldn't help but feel a sense of relief. Although, he did feel guilty for that feeling. Todd climbed into the back seat of a social worker's car. The social worker looked at him with empathy.

"I guess it must have been scary here without any neighbours living for miles around to even run to."

"There is a man that lives less than a mile away," Todd said.

"I lived and worked in this area for a long time. No one lives near here," the social worker said.

Todd pointed in the direction of Chris's house. "There is a house down that way that's been there for a long time. Some people of Native American descent."

The social worker looked at him confusedly. "There was a house there where an elderly lady and her middle-aged daughter lived. But the grandmother died, and the daughter killed herself after having a stillborn son. No one knew who the father was. The house was torn down by relatives."

"Let's get you out of here. I know a place with other kids like you. I think you're going to like it."

As they rode away, Todd looked at the upstairs window of his room. For a moment, he could swear he saw his father there, staring at him with overwhelming hate in his eyes.

TRAPPED

I have been trapped in this place for a while. I wasn't sure for exactly how long. All I knew was that I had to get home to feed my dogs. They haven't eaten all day. I actually work at this place. I was a janitor. I cleaned the halls. I had done so for years. I was probably one of the few people who understood how much I did here. I doubt they could replace me and still receive proper quality work.

When I tried to sweep the floor with a broom, some woman took it away from me. I didn't recognize the woman. She was young with red hair and brown eyes. She told me I couldn't work anymore. She said I needed to take a break and didn't need to worry about cleaning anymore. She recommended I sit down.

I went to sit down at the young lady's suggestion, but as soon as I did, I was strapped down and had a hard time getting up again. I am not sure how long I stayed sitting there. I was getting restless. I couldn't get up.

At one point, I was able to get past the straps. I quickly made my way to the nearest exit, but it was locked. I saw another pair of double doors. So I went to try and open them. They were locked too. There was one more set of double doors. I went to them, and they were also locked. I realized then that I was trapped. What was going on? Why would these people keep me here, trapped against my will?

If my family knew what was going on, they would have these people's heads. Two women came up from behind me. They were dressed in matching gray uniforms. They said I needed to sit down. When I asked them why, they said I might fall. I told them I wouldn't. They informed me that I had been drugged with some tampered pudding I had eaten earlier. That would explain why my mind felt fuzzy. I don't know why they would drug me.

I told them I was fine anyway and wanted them to leave me alone. They came off with fake smiles and polite voices, but it was all for show. I asked them to open the door. They said they could not. They said they would get in trouble. So, someone else was in charge, and they were afraid of them.

One of them grabbed my arms from both sides and started pulling me away from the door. At first, I tried to pull away. When that didn't work, I made to hit the smaller girl, but she dodged the blow. I tried to stomp on her foot and lost balance, almost falling backwards. The other girl caught me and pulled me into a chair. She pulled the chair back against a wall and barricaded me in it.

There was a television near where I was sitting that she turned on. I didn't recognize what was on. No doubt it was some propaganda meant to program or pacify me. With the walls painted white, the heavy doors, and the barricaded windows, this place began to look more and more like a prison.

One man showed up, claiming to be my son. He did have the same color hair as my son. But he was taller and older and looked nothing like my son in the face. It must be some sort of psychological trick they were trying to play on me.

They are trying to gain my trust. Well, it was a stupid ploy, and they've lost all my trust. After this stunt, my trust in them was irredeemable.

I told him he was not my son. He tried to argue and convince me that he was. I didn't budge. He hung his head down, shook it, and walked away. He finally gave up on convincing me of such a ridiculous notion.

Then I saw my daughter. My real daughter came in. I saw her through one of the windows. She was talking to a man in a business suit. *She must be giving it to him*, I thought. She has come to get me out of here. Somehow, she had found out what was going on. She smiled as she walked toward me, but it was not a happy smile. It was one of those smiles used to make someone else feel better. She came over, hugged me, and kissed me on the cheek. I smiled at her, took her hand, and said, "Let's go home."

When I said this, her smile immediately faded away. She said we could not. She said I needed to stay here. I asked why, and she said it was for the better. I couldn't believe she was doing this, my own daughter. They had gotten to her as well. Did they pay her? Threaten her? I was not sure. I was irate and demanded she take me home. She started to cry and turned away, saying, "I cant. I have to go. I love you." She then walked off. I called for her to come back, but she didn't even turn to look at me. She kept walking. They let her out, and she left.

I had to get out of here. I kicked and wiggled until I escaped the trap they put me in. I got up and heard a high-pitched ringing noise. They must have had some kind of alarm on the trap in case I escaped. I saw someone in a gray uniform running towards me. I started to pick up the pace towards the door my daughter had gone out of. I saw a table with some books and crayons on them. I took my hand and swept them on the floor between me and my pursuer.

"No!" she yelled.

I was getting close to the door and ran harder. I came right up to it when I lost balance again.

I fell to the hard floor. Pain shot from my hip down my leg and up my lower back. It was excruciating. My pursuer came up from behind me.

"Are you okay, Mr. Robinson? Are you hurting anywhere?"

I told her where. A woman came out dressed in a blue uniform. She had a machine on wheels with her. She put a device around my arm that squeezed. As if I wasn't in enough pain already.

"This is why we don't want you to get up unless someone is with you, Mr. Robinson. We don't want you to fall. You can't walk by yourself. I am going to call the doctor."

Suddenly, it came back to me. Not all of it but enough. I was in a facility full of nurses and caretakers. I was an eighty-year-old man. I had been diagnosed with Alzheimer's. That is why my mind and memories were fuzzy. My dogs… I wasn't sure what had happened to them. Perhaps my kids had them. Perhaps they were no longer alive. They took me to get an X-ray; luckily, nothing was broken. I did have a bad bruise on my right hip, however. I went to sleep that night.

I woke up in a strange place. My hip was sore. I think I may have had surgery on it not too long ago. I needed to get to a hospital to get it checked out. I got out of bed, and a strange high-pitched ringing went off. An older woman in a peculiar gray uniform ran into the room and told me I needed to lie down and rest. She told me it was the middle of the night, and nothing was open. I was sure that was a lie. I was certain it was late morning. Who was she to tell me what to do?

HERO

This country has taught its people to rely on the law to fight their battles when the baddies threaten them. But what happens when the law lets them down? Many are so dependent on the law they do not know what to do in those situations. The soldiers of the law have so many rules they must abide by that they are incapable of stopping many crimes. But what should be done if a citizen tries to help the law out or pick up the slack the law seems incapable of carrying? This citizen risks the law coming after them and turning them into the enemy. The law has made me their enemy.

It started with their inability to protect my mother from my father. He would beat her, and the police would be called out to the house occasionally by a concerned neighbour. Every once in a while, they would take him away, but he always came back the next day. A judge once told him he was not allowed to return to our home, but he simply ignored the command and came back anyway. The police had no documents stating he couldn't be there when they were called to remove him, so he stayed. My mother lived in constant fear and was too afraid to leave. He knew everyone in her family and where they lived, and he threatened the lives of anyone who offered her a place to stay. He also threatened her that she would never see me again. He said he would plant drugs on her and make sure the police caught her with them, ensuring she would be declared an unfit parent.

That was when I learned the law was not really a protective force for citizens. It was a tool the powerful manipulated against the less powerful.

Of course, there were the heroes. That's what people called them anyway. They rescued people during catastrophic events, such as hurricanes, nuclear fallout, and even mass shootings. But the average Joe was on his own against petty crimes in the small, everyday neighbourhoods of rural America. This made sense. I didn't blame the heroes. They had their gifts and powers. They were too powerful to help people like me. They were more useful in protecting massive crowds of people from disastrous events.

I have always admired heroes and what they do. I always thought that troubled towns and families should have their own heroes, even if they were less powerful. I met an older man in my trailer park with trophies and pictures of himself in some martial art tournament. I later learned it was for a taekwondo tournament. He was a black belt with two stripes. He had been in it for over a decade. He told me he would take me under his wing and teach me everything he knew.

I started going over to his house after school. He had me do various physical exercises, like pushups on my knuckles and fingers. I even trained on an old punching bag he hung up behind his trailer. He made me repeatedly hit my shins and forearms with a stick, and I had to slap wooden posts into the ground with my palm, the backs of my hands, and the ridge of my hands. He told me it would make them hard and tough. I practised katas, kicks, and strikes every day. I also started lifting weights in the school's gym. After several months of this, I took a homemade mask and hood and put them over my head. I took a knife, which was really more of a throwing knife, and slid it into a knife holster on my side.

Mom was out working late. It was dark. I went to the front door of our trailer and unlocked and opened it with my spare key. The man who called himself my father was watching TV with a beer can in his hand.

"Get out," I told him in as firm and confident a voice as I could muster, although it wasn't much.

He looked at me, scanning me up and down. His eyes came to rest upon my face, and a grin slowly emerged on his face. He laughed and said, "What is this? Thoth? Ha! You look as dorky as your name. You are dorky. Do you think I wouldn't recognize you through that ridiculous mask? Stop acting like a pussy and get out of my sight."

"No," I said. "You are going to leave now."

I could feel the anger inside me building up as he taunted me. Laughing at me like I was a joke. I must be a fool even to attempt to stand up to him. But I had decided I would make him leave no matter what, even if I had to break the law. The law was broken anyway. I could not rely on it. It was up to me to make things happen that the law was powerless to change. Fueled by my anger, I repeated myself more confidently and firmly, "You are going to get your shit and leave right now, and you will never return."

His face lost its grin. He stood up slowly. "Oh, yeah? If I left, what would your poor mom do? Where would this family be without me?" he asked.

"What? The money you bring in selling dope?" I asked. "Mother already has to work overtime to keep us up, including you. I'd say that without you here, sitting on your ass and hogging up resources, our ability to make ends meet would be about even. I'm willing to bet we'd be better off financially in addition to the peace of mind we would have."

He spat at me and said, "Fuck you. I ain't going anywhere. You'll have to kill me first."

I narrowed my eyes and said, "You sure you want to make that invitation? It would be easier not to worry about you if you were six feet under."

He waved his hand at me dismissively, clearly conveying that my thoughts didn't matter. He sat back down on the couch and started to ignore me. I picked up a beer can off the kitchen counter next to me.

"I guess you didn't hear me. I said LEAVE!"

I threw the can at his head, rocking his head back a little. He stood up and charged at me. I quickly sidestepped and brought my arm up in line with his neck, putting enough force behind it to knock him over backwards. He made to get back up, and as soon as he had stood up all the way, I snapped a front kick to his face. The back of his head hit the edge of the kitchen counter. He was obviously dazed and seemed to be fighting to stay conscious. I pulled the knife from its holster and pushed the blade against his neck.

"You are going to be out of here in the next ten minutes. Take all the stuff belonging to you that you can. If you miss anything, tough shit. I don't care where you go. I don't care if you have to sleep on the streets for the rest of your life. You are not getting sympathy from me. You will not return here. If you do, I will not go so easy on you. In fact, I will kill you. I do not care if I go to prison for the rest of my life. I just do not care anymore. Do you understand me?"

He nodded his head weakly. He slowly stood up. He grabbed the rest of his beer out of the fridge and a baggy of weed he kept under the couch cushion. He snatched some clothes and a few other things and went outside into the night. That was the last time I ever saw him.

When my mother got home, she asked where he was. I said he had left and was not coming back. I do not know if she ever ran into him after that. If she had, she never told me.

The feeling I got after that incident was extraordinary. Taking control of my own destiny. Helping my mother. Serving justice that had been long overdue. I felt good about myself. It felt good that I had accomplished something and solved my own problems despite it being scary at first. I wish everyone could feel the way I felt.

But they can't. Many people around me were being oppressed by those using fear. And they couldn't do anything about it for fear of both their oppressors and the law. Maybe I could help more people like me. I could continue chasing this feeling and help make more people's lives better. I needed to work on improving my disguise first. I needed to make myself harder to identify and more anonymous.

After getting a few things at a thrift store, my disguise was ready. It covered my face from just below my eyes down to my neck. I also wore a front-brim hat low enough to cast a shadow over my eyes. I also wore gloves. The rest of the suit was made of leather for a bit of protection. It was all a dark blue color. I decided to do my first rounds after the sun went down.

I knew of one place in a bad part of town behind a closed-down gas station. It was on the edge of downtown, and people in the neighbourhood without automotive transportation had to walk through that spot. Rough people would hang out here at night. It was rumoured to be a gang. One man had reported being beaten up and robbed. And two ladies had reported being sexually assaulted. The police, of course, did nothing about it. I came around a curve and saw the dead gas station ahead of me. Some guys were standing around in the back. They were drinking alcohol, and it looked like one had just snorted a line of cocaine.

"HA HA HA," they laughed. "What are you supposed to be, The Masked Lone Ranger?" one of them said.

"Just wearing what I like. It's a free country," I responded.

"That's a rude way to answer the question. We were just making light of a dumb situation, that's all," one guy said. He wore a blue bandanna on his head and another around his neck like a tie. He also wore a jean jacket and boots. He started walking towards me, and two other guys flanked him a little behind on either side.

"You are right though. This is a free country. But this here is our turf. And we wish to exercise our freedom to express responses to stupidly dressed assholes."

He brought out a switchblade knife, flipping out the blade and holding it in front of him. The other two guys raced around him and grabbed my arms, one on each side of me. I took my right foot, brought it up against the one on my right's shin, and stomped it down hard on his foot. The pain caused him to loosen his grip on my right hand, so I twisted and pulled it away. As I did this, I rotated the left guy's wrist in my hand, grabbed his elbow with my right hand and twisted it, forcing him to let go. I then took both hands, pushed his arm up behind his body, and shoved him away. I backed up away from all of them.

"Oh, the Lone Ranger's got some moves," they taunted.

At this point, I began to realize the weight of the situation I had gotten myself into. Three people were on me all at once, and more poured in behind them. My life was really in danger, and I was in over my head. I wasn't going to go down without a fight though.

I slid my knife out of its holster and threw it at the guy with the knife. It stabbed into his thigh. He dropped his knife and sat down, hollering in pain. As the guy closest to me looked at his friend and turned to look back at me, I threw a spinning back fist aimed at his temple but missed and hit his nose instead. His eyes began to water, and he tackled me. He held me to the ground and started beating me, alternating back and forth between my stomach and face. The second guy picked up the knife on the ground and walked towards me.

Then I heard a voice coming from above my head to the right. "Now, is that any way to treat someone you have just met?" it asked. I looked toward the sound, as did everyone else. It was an older man in a long jacket that hung down below his knees. He had a round-brimmed hat.

"Get out of here, grandpa. Unless you think you have lived life for too long? We can help you with that," the man on top of me said.

The older man smirked and said, "You young people do not respect yourselves anymore. You don't take care of yourselves and get the proper amount of sleep that you're supposed to. It is so late. You really should be in bed right now; it is healthy. So why not take a nap."

Everyone in that parking lot, except for him and me, fell unconscious.

We sat at a waffle house nearby. He wanted to take me out to dinner and talk. After what I saw him do, I couldn't say no. I had taken off my mask and gladly followed him. He said he admired my spirit. I fought even when I had lost all hope.

"That's the kind of spirit every hero needs," he said.

"Well, I ain't no hero," I said. "After that whole fiasco, I have learned that. I need to stay in my place and leave the hero-ing to the heroes. People with powers and abilities."

Superpowers. That is what I needed. But I wasn't lucky enough to get hit by some radioactive waste like Osiris, or be part of some scientific experiment gone wrong like Horus, or be from another planet like Isis. It just wasn't in the stars for me. I guess I should count myself lucky I was able to be a hero to my mom.

"Your first mistake was going around and looking for a fight. That is not what heroes do. That is more akin to the role of a villain. You were looking for excitement, not to help people," the stranger said.

"I wanted to help people. Those guys have done some bad stuff to people, and the authorities are too scared to do anything about it. I wanted them to think twice before they continued to prey on the innocent and weak. You don't know what my intentions are. You don't know anything about me." I responded defensively. "Small-time people like us can't rely on heroes to come to help us. We can't even rely on cops."

"Well, what you did for your mother was heroic. It was also brave to stand up to a man that had terrorized you for so long," the man said.

I gasped. "How did you know…? Have you been stalking me, watching me?"

The man laughed. "No, I didn't have to do that. I see it as a strong memory you carry. One you are proud of, and you should be," he said.

"So you have powers. Well, why are you not out helping the heroes? I think knocking people out with some words and reading minds would be useful."

The man smiled slightly. "I help the heroes in my own way. I just help in a way that is not in the spotlight. I have a different role to play. You have the potential to be a great hero," he said.

"I have no potential. I have no powers. Without powers, I just scream at corruption and cuss at those who prey on the weak. But it does nothing. Anyway, how did you get your powers?" I asked.

"It takes more than powers to be a hero. You have to care. You have to care for the innocent. You have to care when lives are in danger. You have to pity those under the rule of corruption. You have to be angry at those who prey on the weak. You must not be indifferent to such things, no matter how much you have seen them or how normal it may begin to feel or how powerless you may think you are. Those are characteristics you have," the man said. "I have been out looking for potential heroes to take on the mantle. I believe you are a good candidate."

"A good candidate? Like I said, I have no powers. What, are you looking to make an army of nobodies so they can die on the frontlines while heroes are in the background doing what they do? Are you their recruiter?" I snapped back.

The man leaned forward. "You asked how I got my powers. I got them like everybody else. I trained for them. I worked for them. People think that heroes are lucky. People dream of being heroes, saying 'if only'... They believe maybe one day they will get lucky and fate will smile at them during some serendipitous event that will grant them superpowers. Just like that, their lives will change forever without having to put in any work or effort," he said.

"Of course, the government would have studied how superpowers worked and be able to duplicate that in other people. Then they just train them, right?" I asked.

"No, the government would love to, but we don't allow it. The truth is, everyone has powers, including you. They are just latent inside you. In most people, they remain dormant. We come from an age-old secret society that has learned how to bring these abilities out of people. There are some people outside of our society who stumble on their powers. When this happens, people think they are haunted or that God helped them and performed a miracle. Sometimes people realize the miracles came from them, and they'll turn it over to make a profit, performing shows as psychics or small-time magicians," he said.

He then told me, "How do people know the stories about how the heroes got their powers? Have you heard any of them tell anyone? They are just rumours. Of course, the heroes don't deny the rumours and actually encourage them sometimes. This satisfies people's curiosity and throws them off the scent. Only those who are worthy should know their powers can be developed and be shown how to do it. I am not just a recruiter. I am a trainer. I train heroes. You trained in taekwondo. You put in all you had to be a hero with it. I am hoping you will put that same spirit and attention into training to be a hero. That is if you accept the offer I am presenting to you."

"What if I said no? I could tell the public everything you just told me. Would you try to make it look like I was crazy?" I asked.

"I would know if that were your intention, and I would wipe your memory of this entire conversation. Actually, that is what I would do if you rejected the offer whether or not you intended to tell the public. But I know you are not going to turn down the offer. It is a once-in-a-lifetime offer. So in a sense, you did get lucky and have the opportunity to get powers," he said.

"Ok, I want to do it," I said.

He smiled and said, "Good, now finish your patty melt. Go home and tell your mom that a job opportunity has come up. I will take you to where you will be staying for the next several years," he said. "By the way, my name is Anubis."

"Job opportunity? She is going to wonder about school," I said.

"Fine, tell her an opportunity has come up for you to attend a school for special people that could help you get a good job," he responded.

The next morning we drove for a few hours until we reached a private beach where a small boat awaited us. There was a man who looked like he was in his early twenties and a girl who looked about my age, sixteen or seventeen. They seemed to have been brought there by an older man and woman as well.

We rode in the boat until almost dusk. I talked to the two recruits I rode with and learned the man's name was Seth. He was from Oregon. The girl's name was Hathor, and she was from Ohio. We talked about meeting our recruiters and what we thought we were getting ourselves into.

Anubis cut in on our speculation and started to tell us about powers. He said they were all the same and worked the same way. As you advance, they can manifest in different ways. It was believed the powers came from using some sort of life energy or psychic energy that was everywhere on the planet. It surrounds and penetrates every living and nonliving thing. Some people have temporarily experienced being one with it during advanced training. Anubis says it puts them in a state of ecstasy when they experience it. It can affect the Earth's electromagnetic field. Or perhaps it is a part of the Earth's electromagnetic field. Either way, heroes are able to manipulate the field to affect matter or shoot lightning like Isis, or create heat and fire like Osiris.

He said sensing the energy could help you read people's thoughts and intentions, which seemed to affect the energy. Because of this, strong emotional distress and even death could cause changes in the energy anywhere on Earth. Learning to sense this would allow you to immediately know if someone was in danger or dying, especially if you loved the person and were attuned to their energy.

The boat took us to a private island with mountains in

the distance and lots of forests. We took a cobblestone path that led to a place resembling an old Buddhist monastery. Flower gardens and bonsai trees peppered the maze of pathways going around and through the institute. The different small buildings had distinctive Japanese-looking architecture, but the roofs were pyramid shaped. There were small shiny white pyramids scattered through the gardens. A vegetable garden in the back grew very pretty, healthy-looking vegetables. Behind this was an orchid of fruit trees and berry bushes. People were tending to the gardens and fruit trees.

"This will be the source of your food while you are here," Anubis said. "You will mostly eat fruits and vegetables. We also have a building where we grow mushrooms and fishermen who catch fish several times a week."

"With all the training we will be doing and this energy we will be learning to utilize, won't we need to take in more calories?" I asked.

"You will have plenty of food, just not the kind you're used to. But since you bring it up, you will be fasting once a week. Contrary to your reasoning, we have found that taking in less food and fasting helps to hone our abilities. The energy you utilize is taken from your environment, so you do not need to worry about producing it. Fasting and eating fewer calories will also increase your ability to focus. I suppose it goes back to when we hunted for food. When you are hungry, your brain needs to focus more on finding food."

Anubis showed me to the room where I would be sleeping. Then he showed us the rather small cafeteria. Lastly, he took us to the auditorium where we would be training. It was huge and the biggest building on the island by far. It was made of cement bricks, unlike the other buildings. It also had a pyramid-shaped roof.

He told them that certain places on Earth seemed to be

good conductors or concentrators of the energy. This island was one of them. A tribe that used to live on the island told stories of healing springs, divine visions, and dreams that told the future.

"The first thing you will do in your training is to learn to sense the energy. This is the foundation of what you will learn after," Anubis told us.

"Will we get to meet the heroes, like Osiris and Isis? Do they live here?" I asked.

"They have houses on the other side of the island. They are more like vacation homes, however. The heroes generally live near the places they protect. Once you learn levitation, it is easy to get to and from the island. They do stop by periodically, though. So you will get a chance to meet them," Anubis answered.

"I can't wait. I am a huge fan of theirs," Hathor commented.

"When do we start training?" I asked.

"Ambitious one you got there, Anubis," replied one of the other recruiters.

"That is what we are here for," I said.

"We will start in the morning. Each of you will train one-on-one with your recruiters until you get the hang of things and start developing independently. Then you will have training sessions together. You will help each other hone and strengthen your powers. Initial separation will also reveal how the power will manifest in its own way with each of you," Anubis said. "It has been a long trip today. Eat some dinner and get some rest. You have a long day tomorrow."

"Focus and concentrate, but relax," Anubis told me. We had eaten an apple that morning and had started training right away. First, I meditated on my breath.

"Relax your body first, then you can start concentrating," Anubis said.

After a couple of hours of doing this and alternating between some sort of slow body movement and stretching, I finally began to feel something; a tingling sensation in the palms of both my hands. I could feel a ball of resistance, like an invisible force field, in between my hands as I alternated between spreading them apart and bringing them together. The force seemed to oscillate between expanding and contracting as I did this.

After a few more hours, the tingling intensified, feeling like electricity vibrating throughout my body. This was the first time I sensed the energy. It was hard to contain my excitement, but I had to. As soon as I felt excitement, the sensation would go away. The moment I felt this energy, I knew it was true. I could be a hero. I could develop powers just like them.

I progressed pretty quickly throughout the next few weeks. I learned to sense random targets. I learned to move a hanging needle inside of a glass ball. I was able to make a compass go crazy. I even succeeded in setting a leaf on fire in my hand. I had good and bad days, finding some tasks easier to pick up than others. But overall, I had become pretty good at developing the power in a short period of time. At least, I felt I was moving along faster than was expected.

A few months passed, and it was finally time to train with the other apprentices in the auditorium. My most significant power so far was the ability to create illusions. Only simple ones though. I could make things look like something else of a similar size and shape. For example, I could make a flamingo look like a baby giraffe, or a pipe look like a stick.

Anubis said that with time and practice, I would be able to create illusions from nothing. I could even make people hallucinate whole worlds.

The idea was exciting until I met up with the others. Hathor had been able to set fire to a fire pit using only her powers, and Seth managed to knock his instructor out for a time. I felt I got cheated on my powers, and I was falling behind.

In the auditorium, we practised using our powers on one another. It was like a competition of sorts. With practice, Hathor managed to light ten small candles one after the other in quick succession. She did this while I held the candles in my hands. In the last couple of rounds, she did this without burning me too badly. Seth remarked sarcastically how useful the ability would be if the power went out. She then set the back of his mullet on fire. One of the instructors put it out with his mind and healed the burns on the back of Seth's head.

Seth "shot" some sort of psychic ball at me, causing me to feel dizzy to the point where I thought I was going to pass out. The world spun, my vision blurred, and it felt like a darkness was covering me, threatening to overtake me completely. I just managed to pull myself from it.

"You have a strong will," Anubis told me since I didn't pass out from Seth's attack. I then made the unlit candles look like they were all lit up. I pushed it further and made those flames appear to spread throughout the auditorium. It was the greatest presentation of power I had done yet. Perhaps the competition helped drive me. I was pretty proud and felt very powerful, but Seth laughed and said it wasn't much better than a magic trick.

Anubis said, "You have all done very well today. You saw how working together helped develop each of your abilities. During your training, we will also focus on teamwork. You will have to work in teams on some missions. We do have good news. Both Osiris and Isis will be visiting us tomorrow. They will talk to you a little about their experience and offer words of encouragement. You will be able to ask any questions you have of them."

"Yes! I can't wait," Seth said.

The next day we all met in the auditorium. Osiris and Isis were there, dressed in normal clothes and looking every bit like normal people. Except that they looked extra confident and strong. It was strange not seeing them in the uniforms they usually wore on television and social media.

"Welcome, future heroes of the planet. It is a huge responsibility, and you need to take it seriously," Osiris began. "Do not think your training is only about developing power. It is about developing character. These abilities are a means to an end, not an end in themselves." The speech was given like he had it memorized and planned out.

Isis went on to say, "Yes, and do not let the power you develop go to your heads. You are not gods. It can be easy to do. When I was growing up, I was bullied in school. The people who bullied me would beat me up, destroy school projects I worked hard on, and ruin anything I openly cared about. I was repeatedly embarrassed in front of the school. After developing enough powers to start going out on missions, I felt pretty powerful. I felt like I could do anything, like nobody could touch me."

"One day, we went to help people during the massive earthquake that hit New York city. On an antenna falling from the top of a tall building was the main guy who daily led the group of bullies against me at school. I saw him, and those memories and that anger resurfaced. I floated near him, looking into his eyes. I wanted to just leave him there to fall to his death. Better yet, I could kill him myself. There were no witnesses around. No one would ever know what happened to him. I looked into his eyes, and he looked into mine. He didn't know who I was, but there seemed to be a slight flicker of recognition in his eyes. I overcame my emotions, flew over, and carried him to safety."

"The life you had before coming here is over. You cannot let injustices then, or even injustices that happen to you in the future, get in the way of making the right decisions. It may be tempting. But you must learn to forgive and put helping people above your own feelings," Osiris finished.

"Do you have any questions for us?" Osiris asked.

"I am just so psyched to meet you. Could I get your autographs? I have the books you wrote and a pen right here. Please let me get your autographs," Seth insisted.

"Sure," they both said simultaneously. They took his pen and signed the book.

That evening during dinner, they both started to feel extra tired and decided to stay in their rooms and sleep. The next morning they were both found dead.

It turns out Horus hadn't come to the island because no one could get a hold of him. The reason being he was also dead. He was found in a room at an event he attended. He died quietly in his sleep as if from poison, just like Isis and Osiris.

That afternoon, the day Osiris and Isis had been found dead in their beds, black helicopters flew over the island. Small motor boats with people carrying AK47s and M16s landed on the island's shores. There were no insignias on their uniforms or on the air and watercraft. A man rappelled down from a low-flying helicopter and walked to the centre of a big garden that was in the middle of the school. He brandished a powerful megaphone. Everyone was surprised. This was not expected, and no one knew who they were. This was particularly surprising given that the island was full of people with psychic abilities.

The man on the megaphone announced, "This island is now being occupied by the Titans. Your heroes are gone. You can surrender now or be killed!"

I heard the sound of gasps all around me. Anubis grabbed my arm and said, "Come." He led me to a garden with tall statues. He went to the base of one statue and pressed the toenail on the left foot's big toe. It was a hidden button that opened a secret door. We ran down a corridor that opened up into a large room. Seth, Hathor, and their instructors were already there.

Seth was sweating. He looked scared. He couldn't stand still.

"We have been trying to investigate a group called the Titans," Anubis said. "We didn't know what their plans were, but we knew they intended to eliminate the heroes and anyone else with powers. They seemed to have found a way to hide their plans and minds from us, putting up "cloaked" thoughts to hide their true thoughts. I guess they have succeeded in their plan to assassinate the heroes. Which is precisely why we needed replacements. We realized we might need backup just in case they succeeded. Unfortunately, we didn't have as much time as we thought."

"Why do they want to kill the heroes?" I asked. "And how did they kill Osiris and Isis? They were here all day yesterday, and everything seemed fine."

"They seemed to have been poisoned," one of the instructors replied. "It may have been an inside job. It could have been anybody."

I watched as a drop of sweat slowly ran down Seth's forehead. He wiped his brow.

"Perhaps you guys have been relying on your powers for so long that y'all aren't too good at reading body language. Seth is acting like he knows something," I said.

"Shut up!" he yelled. "You're right. I am the one who did it. I killed Osiris and Isis. There was a needle in my pen. It's so thin it's like a mosquito biting you. You're unlikely to feel it. Our group designed nanocrystals that bind psychic energy so it can't be read or used. It was in the poison, so no one would sense the poison. Someone else killed Horus while I was here. I lead my group to this island, but we have more spies here. That is why we knew you were looking for replacements. The perfect opportunity for infiltration. No one should have the kind of power Isis or Osiris have. That anyone here has. That is why the Titans have been working to keep people ignorant of latent powers. You heard Isis. He was tempted to kill a guy who bullied him back in high school. No one should have these abilities. They are too dangerous."

Seth continued, "You all are a terror to this world. People live in fear, in…" Seth stopped abruptly. His face went pale, and he dropped to the floor. One of the instructors bent down and felt his wrist for a pulse.

"He is gone," he said.

"I stopped his heart," Anubis said.

The other instructor gasped. "We do not kill, Anubis."

"All is fair in love and war, and this is war," Anubis said. "Besides, we do not have time to listen to his fanatical rambling. You should have been wiser in choosing your recruit."

"He seemed like the perfect candidate," Seth's instructor said.

"Follow me," Anubis said.

He led us down a long corridor with a secret door attached to the auditorium. We ran up a spiral staircase to a small room with walls made of glass. We were on the roof of the auditorium, and we could see for miles around.

People were struggling. Some were going with the Titans, and some were fighting back. Some people who surrendered were executed, while others were taken away. It looked like a military invasion. The people who were fighting back were being shot at. Some areas of the school were even being bombed.

"I have an idea," I said. "Hathor, set the tiki torches on fire. Light them up."

"What? Why?" Hathor asked.

"Trust me," I said.

She lit them up. She also set a small reed bench on fire, but it burned out.

"Anubis, can you telepathically tell everyone who belongs here to act like they are burning, in pain, and even dying?"

Anubis smiled in recognition. He knew what I was thinking. "Yes," he said.

"I am going to start at one of the buildings that got blown up," I said. I created illusions of a fire spreading quickly to consume the whole school. The people started screaming in agony and convulsing.

"Hathor. Set actual fires near the invaders so they can feel the heat and burn," Anubis told her.

She did this, and the invaders took off. They fled the conflagration in their helicopters and boats, retreating from the island. Unfortunately, they did take some prisoners. I continued to make it look like the fire spread all over the school and beyond. I made the forest surrounding us look like it was all lit up too. I conjured illusions of the island spewing smoke into the air. I continued this for thirty minutes to ensure the invaders were out of sight.

After the event, Anubis complimented me on my leadership and for pushing my power beyond my comfort zone in our time of need. He said he made a great choice choosing me as a recruit. One of the instructors decided to take it to a board of elders that he had killed Seth. The board of elders acted like the judges and politicians of the island. They decided to exile Anubis. This was supposed to be a more lenient punishment than putting him in a coma, which was the alternative choice. Because of his years of service to the school (he had even taught Isis), they gave him the lesser sentence. However, he was not to use his powers. If he ever did, they would know and be forced to put him in a coma. I do not understand how a coma is better than death. It seems practically the same to me.

They appointed a new instructor and sent him out to find a recruit. Seth's instructor, Apophis, became my instructor. Hathor and I have continued to work together to progress our powers. We are working much harder. We knew it was only a matter of time before the Titans figured out what had happened and returned with another attack, stronger and wiser.

But I am becoming wiser and stronger too. I can feel myself becoming more powerful. I am beginning to feel like a god. After all, am I not becoming one? One day I will hit a high enough level that no one will be able to touch me. No one will be able to do anything to me…

THE MUSHROOM TRAP

Her name was Patricia. I met her in my microbiology class in college. She was kind, intelligent, and beautiful and I fell head over heels for her the day I met her. Everyone at school who knew her liked her, so I figured I didn't stand a chance. She did go out of her way to talk to me and be my lab partner, but I figured that was just the kind of person she was.

Patricia and I were both biology majors. I loved microbiology the most, with fungi being one of my favourite subjects. The microbiology instructor, Mr. Ivan Wilbanks, wasn't that much older than us and was a relatively new instructor at the school. Mr. Wilbanks seemed to show Patricia extra attention. I suspected he had ulterior motives. Sometimes as Patricia and I walked out of class together he would strike up a conversation with her. I always figured it was none of my business, so I would leave the class and let them have their moment.

One time he did this, he talked to her about mushrooms and showed off a picture of some he was growing. I saw the picture and asked, "Are those oyster mushrooms?"

"Yes," Mr. Wilbanks replied. "Are you interested in mushrooms?"

"Yes, very much," I said. "I believe we are only beginning to see their true potential. There's still so much to learn about their effects on the ecosystems around them."

"I grow a bunch of them at home. I was just showing these fine specimens to Patricia here," Mr. Wilbanks said.

"Yes, he was telling me about the cool setup he has at his house and wants to show me more of his mushrooms," Patricia said. "Maybe Gabe can come to see them too. He does have an interest in this stuff."

"I would love to," I said.

"Sure. If y'all want, you can come by my house on Saturday. You can come meet some of my mushroom children," he joked awkwardly. We all exchanged numbers, and he texted over his address, saying he would see us on Saturday morning.

I arrived at his house on Saturday. It was a modest home out in a rural area. His yard looked like the garden was left to its own devices as it had gone a little wild. Patricia was already there. She motioned me over to a large shed in the garden. I went over and came inside.

There was a flow hood inside and some petri dishes lying around. Alcohol bottles and mushroom grow bags sat on top of a mini fridge, and a table with an alcohol lamp stood at the centre of the shed. Different types of substrates for growing mushrooms were packed on shelves and hanging from the ceiling. Mushrooms were even growing from a tree stump in a corner of the shed. It looked like organized chaos.

"So, I want to show you something that you will not find anywhere else, but you must not speak of it to anyone. I do not have a license or the approval to work with these types of mushrooms, and the red tape to officially be able to do so is a nightmare. But it is all done in the name of science."

"I can respect that," I promised. Patricia agreed.

"I have found a way to combine the DNA from psilocybin and fly agaric mushrooms. I've already talked to Patricia about it. How do you feel about psychedelics, Gabe?" Mr. Wilbanks said.

"I think they have a lot of potential for medicinal advancements and for treating mental health. They could even help us study and understand consciousness," I said.

"Well, this new mushroom hybrid has psychedelic chemicals from both fly agaric and psilocybin. It makes the experience at least ten times more intense than either chemical could induce by itself," Mr. Wilbanks said. "I tried it, and it felt like I was taken to another world. A world with pink skies and clean-smelling air. I found myself in a meadow covered with grass and flowers. There were also giant mushrooms. Some mushrooms were bigger than me, almost the size of small trees. I found one mushroom that even had a face. It looked like it was sleeping, but I thought it moved a little. The weirdest thing I found was a pond. In contrast to everything else, this pond seemed dark and foreboding. It gave off a creepy vibe. When I stared at it, my curiosity about it deepened. I became completely transfixed, and the world started to fade. Then I came down from the experience.

"It sounds pretty amazing," Patricia said.

"It was," replied Mr. Wilbanks. "I felt like I hadn't taken enough though. The experience didn't last long enough. I figured we could try it at a higher dose. If you guys are up for it?"

"Hell yeah," Patricia replied. "Let's do it."

"If you're not up for it, Gabe, I understand," he said to me.

"I will see what happens to Patricia first, then I will decide," I said.

Ivan took out some already cut-up mushrooms from the

mini-fridge and handed Patricia three. He told her to eat them.

"That seems like a lot," she said.

"I took two, and it wasn't long enough," he said.

Patricia shrugged her shoulders and ate them. After a few minutes, Patricia said she needed to sit down. It wasn't long before she started smiling and laughing at nothing. Eventually, she just stared off into space, completely oblivious to everything around her. She then closed her eyes, laid back, and went still.

Ivan and I talked for about an hour. Patricia still never came to. We tried waking her, but she did not respond. Thankfully, her pulse felt good and clear when Ivan checked.

"There is only one thing to do," Ivan said. "One of us needs to take some mushrooms and see if we can get her out."

I looked at him in disbelief. "How is that going to help? You or me taking mushrooms? We need to get her to a hospital," I said.

"No, they will find out what I have been doing," he protested. "Look, there is something I didn't tell you guys. I took the mushrooms twice and saw the same world both times. When I let my brother try some, he saw the same place."

"He saw the same thing because of what you told him," I said. "What are you getting at?"

"No, I never told him about my experience. He saw it anyway. I think it is a real world. Real in some sense. Maybe a world made of mind stuff that these mushrooms can take you to."

"Ok," I said. "We can try it your way, but you need to do it quickly."

"No, you should be the one to do it," he said. "I've seen

how you look at her. This is your chance to be her knight in shining armour."

"Or I could be in a coma beside her needing a hospital too," I said.

"Look, if you are out for ten minutes, I will immediately call for help," he said.

I was sceptical, but I trusted him and agreed to try it.

I took three mushrooms, and the world started to fade away. As the world disappeared, I heard Ivan say, "Don't stare into the pond."

The world that invaded my awareness and replaced my normal, everyday world was gorgeous. Ivan's description had not done it justice. The grass was greener than any green I had ever seen. The flowers were so brightly coloured they almost glowed. There were flowers and mushrooms of colours I had never seen before.

This world was consistent with Ivan's description. I even saw a giant mushroom that looked like it had a face. The mushroom had a red cap, and the eyes on its face resembled Ivan's. The face did not look asleep to me, though. It seemed awake and stared at me expressionlessly.

I looked around and saw a pond. Patricia was standing in it, about waist deep. She was slowly sinking deeper into the pond. The pond seemed to draw my attention.

As it drew my gaze, I saw a man almost to the centre of the pond. He looked like Ivan, only several years younger. He had Ivan's red hair and his eyes. I realized that this must be Ivan's brother. Was he in a coma somewhere?

I resisted looking at the pond, which turned out to be a difficult endeavour. It was as if aliens had landed on the White House's lawn on national television to make their first public contact with humans. It was like trying to resist watching that.

I tried yelling out to Patricia, but she didn't respond. She was in some kind of trance. So I went in after her in the pond, keeping my eyes averted and shut closed as much as possible. I only shot quick glances to ensure I was still going in the right direction. When I reached her, I came up from behind, wrapped my arm around her waist, and tried to pull her back. There was a resistive force pulling her in the opposite direction—pulling her toward the centre of the pond. It made it difficult for me to drag her out. I pulled harder still and heard a loud noise that seemed to shake the environment. It sounded like a roar and had come from the pond's centre. It drew up a great fear in me, spiking an adrenaline rush that enabled me to pull harder and succeed in pulling her from the pond. A dark, gooey tentacle shot up from the centre of the pond. It slithered from the abyss of the dark centre towards the pond's edge, which was a brilliantly bright blue.

The tentacle thing started wrapping itself around Patricia's leg, but when I got to the pond's edge, it squirmed, released its grip, and slithered back into the pond. As we stumbled out of the pond, Patricia faded away. After a moment, the mushroom world started to fade and was replaced by the world I was used to. Patricia was awake and talking to Ivan when I woke up. I looked at the clock. Thirty minutes had passed.

"Did you call 911?" I asked Ivan, remembering that he promised he would call for help if we were not awake in ten minutes.

"You don't have to worry about that. I didn't," he said. "And it's a good thing I didn't. You guys are both alive and well. It would have been a waste of their time. Look, you were able to bring Patricia back. Excellent work!"

"Do you think you could bring your brother back?" I asked

"What do you mean?" he asked.

"I saw your brother almost to the centre of the pond. All I could see was his head. He is almost completely swallowed up by the pond. I assume he is in the same kind of coma somewhere that Patricia was in. I even bet this whole stunt with Patricia and me was planned to see if someone could be brought back," I said.

"You were not part of my original plan," he said. "I was going to see if I could bring her back."

"What?" Patricia yelled angrily. "You meant for all that just happened to happen to me?"

"I wanted to bring you out. I guess I thought it would impress you," he said.

"Oh, my god. I do not even know what to say to that," she said

"You wanted to bring your brother out too, I suppose," I said.

Ivan shook his head. "No, he is gone. Did either of you see the mushroom with the face?" he asked us.

"I did," I said.

It wasn't there the first time I went or when my brother went. It only appeared after my brother reached the pond's centre. I think it is him, or part of him. What is left of him. His body does not just lie unconscious anymore. He is dead."

"You risked my life, then," Patricia said in disbelief.

Ivan looked down in shame.

"Where is the body then? Have you told anyone he is dead?" I asked.

"How could I? I hid it. I buried it under my garden. I can't let people know what I am doing. I am making incredible scientific breakthroughs, exploring other dimensions and the potentials of the mind," Ivan said.

"We have to tell people to prevent this from happening to others," Patricia said.

"No!" Ivan yelled.

"If you won't, then I will!" she yelled back.

Ivan picked up a knife off the table and stabbed Patricia multiple times. I grabbed a scapple near the petri dishes, came up behind him, and slit his throat. I dialled 911 on my cell phone and told them I needed an ambulance. Then I went to tend to Patricia.

"I think I'm dying, Gabe," she said.

"No, you're going to be ok," I reassured her.

"I don't think so," she said. "Can I tell you something?"

"Of course," I replied.

"I was kind of hoping we would get a second date, you know, after this one," she said, smiling slightly. "But I guess not."

"Date? With me?" I asked in disbelief.

"Of course. I kept trying to hang out with you, but you never asked me on a date," she said.

"I didn't think you would be interested in a guy like me," I told her.

She smiled and whispered, "Foolish boy." She then closed her eyes.

I heard sirens approaching. "They're here. See, you're going to be okay. And I will hold you to that second date," I said with tears in my eyes.

However, Patricia was already unconscious. She died on the way to the hospital. So we never got to go out officially. I told the authorities what had happened. They didn't believe such a 'wild tale' as they called it. They believed a different set of events had transpired. They thought it was more likely we all took some "funny shrooms" and went into a state of psychosis that led to Patricia and Ivan being killed. I told them to look for the body of Ivan's brother under the garden.

They looked half-assedly and never found it. I guess they

did not want to commit time and money on the word of some drug user. Ivan's brother remains missing.

I was put into a state mental hospital for my "dangerous delusions." I don't know what happened to the rest of the mushrooms. My life puts a whole new spin on the saying: "Drugs will ruin your life."

PSYCHONICS

He had been running and hiding most of his life. Pursued because he was born with a defect. At least, that is how the Oglichs thought of it. There was a time when his people were admired and respected for their gifts—their "divine blessings", as they had once been called. But when the Oglichs took over, they saw his kind as a threat and called the gifts a dark curse.

The Oglichs had people like him that they used. His people were called Psychonics. He was referred to as Hermes. His people exhibited genetic characteristics that enabled the electromagnetic fields produced by their nervous systems to interact with the planet's electromagnetic field. This gave them particular abilities. Abilities that allowed them to sense and affect their environments in ways others could not, although they did fluctuate during storms and solar flares from their star.

Psychonics could sense other Psychonics. Some were even strong enough to sense where other Psychonics were anywhere on the planet if they focused hard enough. These were the ones the Oglichs found useful.

Hermes was part of a rebel group made up of eighteen Psychonics bent on toppling the Oglich regime. They had learned to reduce the energy produced by the interaction between their own and the planet's electromagnetic fields, so other Psychonics had a difficult time finding them.

Hermes was on a particular mission to steal a powerful weapon. It was hidden and locked up in a cave. The rebel group had a double agent working as a Psychonic for the Oglichs who discovered where they kept it. Apparently, it could destroy cities. They were not terrorists, but they needed leverage.

Hermes made his way to the town of Athens, where a celebration was underway. It was the third anniversary of Psychonics officially being declared illegal, and society made safer. Illegal just for being. By now, they had destroyed all but a few Psychonics. Most of the ones still alive were working for the Oglichs.

People were dancing in bright-coloured clothes as a band played a lively tune. There were animals about as well, both natural and artificial. But Hermes focused on the Oglich guards holding high-powered mobile cannons. The kind of mobile cannons one needed two hands to shoot.

Hermes had two small handheld mobile cannons strapped to either side of his belt. They were smaller and only required one hand to shoot them. It was unusual for anyone who wasn't part of the Oglichs' warrior force to possess any type of cannon. It was also highly illegal. Each member of the force is issued a limited amount of registered cannons. This helped the Oglichs to keep track of them. Hermes took his from two soldiers he killed on a past mission. One cannon from each man.

Hermes wore a dark red hood with a cape. It protected him from the desert climate that covered the equivalent of half their planet. Usually, this blended in well with the local populace, but it may stand out against today's vibrant, festive outfits. It was hard to believe that so many people have come to see Psychonics as evil and the source of their misfortune. Not too long ago, they came to Psychonics for advice, aid in searching for lost things, and healing. Many were once good friends with Psychonics. Now, the Oglichs have so many convinced of our darkness.

On the edge of the crowd, Hermes could see someone scanning and searching the crowd. He could sense the searcher was a Psychonic. At this range, even with Hermes' reduced field, the seeker could no doubt sense him too. But he would have difficulty figuring out who the Psychonic was in this crowd. Although, the outfit Hermes wore may help give him away.

Hermes saw the seeker discussing something with one of the guards before he went to say something to the head soldier. The head soldier picked up his loudspeaker and announced, "It has come to our attention that there is a Psychonic in our midst! No one will be allowed to leave until we identify them and have them in custody!"

This was not good. Hermes would not be able to escape with the crowd. And he would give himself away if he tried to make a run for it. He looked around for a means of escape and saw a spring cart. A traveling show that moved from town to town owned it. It was a device that ran on wheels and was powered by springs. They were fast. Much faster than the wopples the guards rode on.

Wopples were genetically engineered creatures made for riding and working. Most of the creatures used by people were genetically engineered to be perfect for the tasks they were used for. Wopples' backs were even shaped like seats for comfortable riding. They could go for a week without food or water. They sported two kneecaps on each leg, with the lower kneecap acting more like an elbow or a reverse knee. This enhanced their speed and balance. When they ran, they seemed to glide across the land.

The spring cart had curtains for the show, making it the perfect escape device. He got in and wound up the springs. One of the people in the crowd spotted him moving behind the curtains and yelled, "He's trying to escape!" while she pointed at the cart.

The guards took notice and ran towards the cart. One of the guards was about to grab on when Hermes suddenly released a spring that engaged the gears and caused the cart to pop off at great speed.

The soldiers took off after him on their wopples. One met him at the north edge of the crowd where the spring cart was heading. Hermes pulled the lever that controlled the hydraulic system and steered the cart. The cart turned sharply to the left, and Hermes dodged the guard.

Another guard joined the one that Hermes just dodged, and they both set off in pursuit. Initially, they were close enough to the cart to almost reach out and touch it, but the distance between them grew steadily. One of the guards took out a metal ball with a button on it. He pressed the button and threw it towards the cart. The ball ejected fumes behind it, boosting its speed, and fell on the back of the cart. The ensuing explosion tore the back half of the cart into pieces.

Hermes fell out of the wreckage and onto the ground. The guards came up from behind him, aiming their cannons at him. Just as one of the guards was about to fire, Hermes rolled to the side with a cannon in each hand pointed at the guards.

One of the guards gasped. The other yelled, "He has cannons!"

Hermes fired the cannons at both their heads. Brains, blood, and bone shards could be seen spraying behind them from a distance. Nothing was left of their heads.

Hermes fought through his soreness and started to run. He knew there was no time to waste. He saw a lone snoodz, one of the creatures here for the celebration. A snoodz was a lot like a wopple, but it was only sold to the wealthiest. It was slower than a wopple but had fins that enabled it to swim. It also had large wings, and while it could not fly, it could glide over long distances even with a rider.

Hermes jumped on it and kept heading north towards his destination. The Oglich soldiers were not far behind. With their faster wopples, they were quickly gaining on him. Up ahead, there was a canyon. It was very foggy so he could not tell how far across the other side was. It just looked like a cliff he was about to run off of. But he knew there was another side because that was his destination. He kicked the sides of the snoodz with his feet, and it ran off the cliff. He pulled back on its neck and the wings snapped out. Cries went up as the guards stopped at the edge of the cliff.

As Hermes glided, he used his ability to sense the overall shape of the canyon's opposite face. He was struck by the sense of something with great power, so he steered the snoodz in its direction.

They landed on a ledge on the other side of the canyon. Hermes could sense the power just below him. He took a rope hanging from the left side of his belt, tied a loop in it, and laid the loop on the ground. Next, he took out a piece of metal that forked into one long and one short blade. At the other end was the flattened ridge of the metal handle. He stabbed the tool into the ground with the edge of the loop in the space between the pronged blades, anchoring it. He stomped on the flat end of the handle a couple of times to drive it deeper into the ground.

He threw the other end of rope down into the canyon. He climbed down the cliff's side until he found a cave. The arch was perfect. It was most likely man made.

He walked inside reached what looked like a complicated combination lock. On closer inspection, he realized it was a Grecian computer. It had five dials and twelve columns. The dials had to be turned so all the numbers on each column added up to forty-two. It can take a lot of time. If he were a Caculon it would take much less time to solve. Caculons could do all kinds of things with numbers and shapes in their heads in a flash. Hermes did not have this ability. Instead, he used a strategy taught by another member of the rebellion that used a matrix to solve the puzzle. It was still costly on time but faster than trial and error.

As soon as he made the first dial turn, he started hearing rhythmic clicking. It sounded like a timer. There was a time limit; if he did not solve the puzzle fast enough, a trap would probably set off.

He reached the last numbers, and the pace of the clicking began to increase rapidly. He knew he was about to run out of time. He turned it to the last number, and the door opened.

Hermes walked in and saw a pyramid on an altar. It was dark. It was so dark it looked like a three-dimensional void shaped like a pyramid. He reached over to pick it up and experienced an overwhelming power surge through him. It felt hot, and it made him hot. The war was not over, but this was a big step in helping the rebels take down the Oglichs.

MOTHER

We pulled into the parking lot of a small building. It looked as if it had once been a small business. Perhaps a car shop or even a laundromat. My wife, Sandy, and I walked in. It was a nice, fairly spacious room that smelled of sweet incense. There were a variety of tapestries on the wall showing different mandalas and patterns reminiscent of East Asian religions. Single mats were spread out all around the room and against the walls. There was a small kitchen to the left as you walked in. A small bathroom on the far end of the room contained adult diapers. It was January and cold up in the Appalachian Mountains of Kentucky. It was a rural area, and snow from the previous day still covered the ground.

I have been waiting a long time for this experience. I was a teenager the first time I heard of the magic potion called ayahuasca, derived from somewhere deep in the Amazonian jungle. I had read about it in a specialized encyclopedia I found in my local library. It was called Man, Myth, and Magic. Ayahuasca could open up new worlds to those who partake of it. I have read a lot about it since then, but no amount of reading could prepare me for the actual experience.

I found a group online that believes certain psychedelic plants could put you in touch with a spirit or god. They were part of a Native American church that practised such beliefs. I joined and was put in touch with a teacher, considered a type of shaman, who could lead me through the experience.

Only two other people were present when my wife and I arrived. The one guy was meditating, and the other was reading. The teacher was there too and greeted us by name. We were told to find mats to settle on but to make sure we were separated. He did not want us to be near each other during the experience. I went and found a mat over in the corner. It was comfortable, and it was going to be my spot for the weekend.

We would drink ayahuasca tonight, spend the night, and do it again on Saturday. More people started trickling during the afternoon. We were told to follow a special diet a couple of weeks before this journey. Basically, we could only eat fresh fruit and vegetables, and we had to abstain from sexual activity.

People with vastly different life experiences came from all over the country to attend the ceremony. That evening, we made a circle around our teacher. He paced around the room, asking everyone in the circle why they were there and what they hoped to get out of the experience.

I said I had no expectations and just hoped it would show me something beyond this reality. One lady had lost a daughter in the past year and needed help getting through her grieving process. Many people talked about emotional wounds they needed to heal from, and some wanted to learn to love themselves. These were the things "mother ayahuasca", as they called it, could help them with.

After the group-sharing event, we all gathered around a table in the kitchen. On it stood a big bowl of tea.

"It is best just to chug it down," the teacher said.

I drank my cup as fast as possible to avoid tasting it. It tasted bad. It tasted worse than dirt. Some people went to sit on their mats. I sat at first but immediately felt nauseated. I didn't want to throw it up. We each had a puke bucket beside us, just in case. We also wore adult diapers as a precaution. They say the stuff will make you purge. Purge any physical, spiritual, or mental crap you got inside you. Sometimes that can be in the form of laughing or crying. Other times it can be by throwing up or through diarrhoea.

After a few moments, I lay all the way down. I didn't know what to expect. They had music playing in the background. It was slow and relaxing. In one hour, the music would change, and then you could take another half drink if you felt like you needed it. The music was the only way to tell how much time had passed. All our electronics were turned off, and there were no clocks in the room.

The music changed, turning into a woman's rhythmical chanting. I felt nothing, so I got up and drank more of the tea. I then went and lay back down on my mat. When I was comfortable, I put on my eye mask.

The music seemed to get louder, filling the background of the world. The Earth itself seemed to move to its rhythm. Still, I felt nothing for a little bit. I began toying with the idea of getting a third drink.

As I thought about doing this, a spiraling tentacle or serpent thing impressed itself on my consciousness. It wasn't really a visual but something more. At first, it was subtle and gentle. I knew it was there and started thinking at it, striking up a conversation with it without realizing the potion was already working.

I thought, "Should I get another drink?"

"I don't know, should you?" a feminine voice answered.

"Will it help me talk to you?" I asked

She said, "I don't know."

The subtlety disappeared, and the serpentine impression grew stronger very quickly. I could feel it over my body. I got scared, sat up, and took the eye mask off to ground myself.

I then almost immediately thought, "No, this is what I came here for."

I put the eye mask back on and lay back down. The most incredibly powerful feeling swept over me. At first, it seemed terrible, and I swore to myself I would never partake again. I felt hot and started pouring sweat. I had to take my shirt off; it was soaked. My mat was wet. The intense feeling eased off a bit, and I felt transported to a world outside our own. It was a place from where I could see many worlds, including the one I lived in. I felt like our world was something akin to a virtual reality game, and we just forgot it was a game. I also felt everything had patterns in an almost platonic way of viewing the world. Even lives and time followed certain prearranged patterns we could not consciously grasp. There were different ways of experiencing these patterns, different lives, dreams, thoughts, and worlds. But these patterns were the core.

As I came down, I felt wonderful. I felt open and loving toward all the people around me. The world and my life suddenly had so much potential. It was as if I had contacted a god that showed me some divine wisdom.

The next morning, my wife and I drove to an artsy town nearby. All the colours and art seemed extra beautiful. I wanted to get lost in them. The music was wonderful too. I couldn't wait to try the drink again.

That Saturday evening, we talked about our experiences of the previous night and how they had impacted us. Interestingly, everyone described encountering a female deity. I suppose that's why it is called "mother ayahuasca."

I decided to take it easy this time around and drink only one drink. As everyone started getting into the experience, one woman got up and danced with others in the group. I lay in my spot and saw a woman with long black hair appear in the centre of the room. She looked around at everyone in the group. Her head and body curved and twisted like a serpent.

My eyes followed her hypnotizing movement. I realized other people around the room had stopped what they were doing. Everyone was staring at the woman in the centre. Was this really happening? Or was it part of the ayahuasca experience?

The guy beside me said, "Woah, I saw my mother, and then she changed into a Native American woman."

The guy on the other side of him said, "I saw my first wife, and she changed into a Native American woman too."

"My children," the being said in a comforting mother-like voice. Her eyes darted around the room, looking rather reptilian for a second. "Come to me."

We all walked toward her in a hypnotized, zombie-like state. As I got closer to her, I could hear her more in my thoughts.

"Give yourselves to me."

The teacher was the only one not moving closer to the being. He was standing with an almost menacing smile on his face. His arms were widespread. The being gestured, and a table with incense on it moved to the centre of the room. A small altar with a serpent deity statue on its top moved from out of a closet, floating of its own accord. These objects seemed to really be moving. The deity was becoming increasingly more real and no longer seemed like a mere hallucination.

"Come closer, children. Give yourselves to me."

As I came to stand before her, her thoughts melded with my own. It became more and more difficult to tell apart the difference between her thoughts and mine. I got the impression of tentacles made of jungle vines rising in the back of my mind, smothering and swallowing my mind. That was all I could remember of that night.

I woke up the next morning on my mat. I hadn't realized I had fallen asleep. Everyone else was still on their mats too. My wife and some of the other people were still asleep. The guy beside me was already awake and said, "I had such a wild experience last night. It seemed so real. We were worshipping some Native American serpent woman."

I looked at the centre of the room. It was empty. There was no altar or anything of that sort.

One of the girls came out of the kitchen, saying, "The teacher left a note. Some emergency came up. We will not be able to do the therapeutic circle today and talk about our experiences."

"Well, that's just as well. I have a long drive home anyway," one of the guys said.

Everyone started packing up and dwindled out. I was trying to figure out how to interpret the previous night.

I asked my wife what she had experienced. She said she remembered a serpent woman sending love and comfort to her, but she couldn't remember a lot of it. Just bits and pieces.

It sounded similar to what my neighbour and I had experienced. I thought it strange, but it must just be an interesting anomaly.

As we were walking out, I saw the closet that had been closed and locked since we got there was cracked open. It was the closet I saw the altar fly out of in my vision. My curiosity rose, and I went over to peek inside. I gasped.

There was an altar with a small statue of a serpent goddess on top.

On the drive home, we listened to music we had never listened to before. It really moved our minds and souls. We felt comforted and at peace. It was an eternal peace and comfort that couldn't be explained. We know mother ayahuasca will take care of us. We can both feel her in the back of our minds. We welcome her. We live to serve her, and she will take care of us.

THE MOUNTAIN TRAP

The tour group was getting ready to board the Cessna and fly up to a glacier at the top of Mount Denali. Mount Denali is the tallest mountain peak in the entire continent of North America. It was the thing I looked forward to the most during our visit to Alaska. Being on top of the world, away from people and the hustle and bustle. Just us and the wonderful sound of silence.

We had come up to visit some of my wife's relatives. It was the first time I had come to Alaska, and I was loving it. We were joined by a single guy named John and an Australian couple named Adam and Juliet. Australian people love to travel. I see them on almost every tour I have been on around the world.

The pilot, who everyone called Ace, explained that the weather had to meet certain parameters for us to land on the glacier. The weather can get crazy up there pretty quickly. So far, everything was looking good.

He explained we had survival provisions in the back of the plane, which could be reached from the outside. We all climbed aboard, and the plane took off. It was small, and you could feel even the slightest wind changes while we were up in the air. Ace told us about extreme climbers who wanted to climb Denali. Some of them were flown up to a certain spot high up on Denali to be able to climb to the summit.

We got lucky, and Ace was able to land on the glacier. It was beautiful. We wore dark sunglasses so the sun's reflection wouldn't hurt our eyes. There was just white glacier and dark rock peaks all around. There was no life other than for the six of us, not even a growing weed. There was nothing else up there except for the plane. It was completely silent. I had never heard such utter silence in all my life. It was peaceful beyond explanation. It can only be experienced.

After having time to take it all in, we gathered in the plane to head back down. As we took off, the wind started to pick up unexpectedly. Ace was trying to guide the plane to safety, but he soon lost control, and the wind tossed the plane around. We started spinning. I became nauseous, and my wife screamed. We were grasping the sides of the plane's interior to brace ourselves. The plane flew straight for some cliff. My heart dropped. The impact was powerful. My head flew back, and everything went black.

I woke up outside in the snow. A strong cold wind was blowing, chilling me deeply. A giant laceration stretched across my chest and down the side of my body. Curiously it wasn't bleeding. I looked over to my right and saw the plane. It was totaled. At first, I saw no one else. Then I saw John come out from the other side. Followed by Juliet.

"Have you seen your wife or Adam or the pilot?" John asked.

"No," I replied. "You haven't seen them? Oh, my god." I started looking frantically around and shouting, "Amber!" I could feel the worry and fear welling up inside me as I imagined the worst. Tears brimmed in my eyes.

"I have tried the radio. It does not work," John said. "I don't know about the others," he said.

Suddenly a man came over a ridge. He was not part of our party. He was pale, missing an arm, and had one eye closed.

"Looks like we got some new visitors to the mountain," he said, seeming calm.

"We still have a couple of people missing from our party. Have you seen anyone else nearby?" I asked.

The stranger looked down and slowly shook his head. I assumed the man was a climber. But I saw no equipment, and I don't think a one-armed man would be able to climb this mountain.

"Can you help us?" I asked the stranger. "Do you have a way of communicating with anyone?" I assumed he must have some way back down the mountain. He shook his head again.

"I have been on this mountain for a long time," he said. This man was creepy and strange.

"We need to gather the stuff from the back of the plane and see what we've got. Ace said there are provisions and survival equipment in there, and maybe there's a radio," John said.

The stranger laughed. "Survival? You don't have to worry about that. It's too late for that."

"What do you mean?" I asked.

"I mean, you already failed to survive. You are no longer alive. You're dead," he said.

I thought this man must be crazy. Maybe he had been up here and was suffering from some kind of delirium from exposure to an extreme environment.

John got the door opened to the survival stuff. "There is nothing here!" He shouted angrily. "Did the pilot lie to make us feel better?"

"Oh, my god! Where is Adam?" Juliet started crying.

"We don't know, and we can't say yet," I said. "We haven't seen them, but we haven't seen any bodies yet either." Immediately after saying bodies, I realized it had been a mistake.

"Oh, my god! Bodies?" She started crying even harder.

"Well, either your friends are alive and aren't dead like you, or they didn't make it on the mountain. Maybe they didn't survive death. They just weren't that 'lucky'," the stranger said. He made quotation mark gestures with his hands as he said lucky.

"Who are you? What are you doing here?" Juliet screamed at him.

"The name is Charles, ma'am," he told her. "I came adventuring up here and fell from a great height. I woke up with my arm stuck between some rocks, and a small rock shard had penetrated my right eye. Try as I might, I couldn't get my arm loose. I tried for a good part of the day. Finally, I took my knife out and cut my arm off to free myself. I figured it was the only way I had a possibility of surviving. That was before I realized I had already died. That was seventy years ago. I am still here."

"Seventy years?" I asked. "You look like you're in your thirties," I said.

"I was when I died," he said.

"How? What do you eat up here?" John asked

"Don't need to eat. Actually, I can't eat. Nothing to eat up here."

"So you don't get hungry?" I asked.

"I feel hungry. At first, it grew until it was painful. But you get used to the hunger after a while," he said.

"This is completely ridiculous," Juliet said. "None of us are dead. We need to find a way to get rescued."

"I understand you do not want to believe me yet," Charles

said. "If I were in your position, I wouldn't believe me either. I can't get you down the mountain, but I can bring you to where some more people are. They can't get you down the mountain either though. They're all dead too. But it can get lonely up here without each other," he said.

"Okay. Take us to them. Perhaps there is some sanity among your friends at least," John said.

He led us a way down the mountain. "It's a five-mile walk," Charles said. "I saw your plane come down and came to see if there were any people who passed over."

"What if we hadn't?" Juliet asked. "You were just going to freak us out?"

"You wouldn't see me if you were alive. We only see some people who are alive, ourselves. The ones we do see don't respond to us. I suppose they can't see or hear us. Sometimes you see them talking to people who don't seem to be there. I guess some people can't be seen alive or dead."

"Alive or dead?" I asked for clarification.

"I died alone. But some of the people you will meet died in groups, and several members of those groups were never seen again. Maybe they're here but invisible to use. Maybe they went to heaven. We often talk and speculate," Charles said.

I saw some people begin to appear in the distance. We approached them, and they shook our hands. They each introduced themselves. There were eleven people in the group. To our surprise, they all backed up what Charles told us. They all talked about how they died, mostly in plane crashes and climbing accidents.

"Can't we make a fire?" John asked. "It's freezing. We can warm up while we get to know each other."

"No, comrade," one guy said. His name was Alfred. "Fire doesn't work here. I haven't seen a tree, weed, or even a blade of grass since I've been here. No life of any kind except us. Well, I guess you can't count us as life."

"So we just freeze?" Juliet asked.

"I'm afraid so. There is no escaping it, but you get used to it after a while," Alfred answered.

Alfred had been here the longest. He died in a climbing accident in 1830. He had been here almost two hundred years.

"There are trees towards the bottom of the mountain. Can't we get wood from there?" Juliet asked. "No," Alfred replied. "We can't go down that far. I have looked for a path since I have been here, and so have others. Rocks and snow are all we see."

"That and the planes," Charles said. "That's always nice entertainment. Although we can't hear them for some reason. The only sounds we hear are strong winds and our own voices."

"Do any of you happen to be good singers?" another guy asked. "We sing, but it would be nice to hear someone that does it well. A nice musical voice. I have almost forgotten what that sounds like."

We all told him we didn't. Juliet asked where her husband, my wife, and the pilot could have gone. One guy said maybe heaven. John said maybe hell.

"No," Charles replied to John. "I am pretty sure that is where we are. This mountain has us tethered. I guess we haunt this mountain. We are its ghosts," Charles continued.

Time dragged by on that mountain, but time did pass. Every several years a few new faces showed up after dying on the mountain. While I felt bad for the poor new souls that got trapped there, I was also guiltily delighted. It was nice to have new people to talk to, to tell us how the world had changed.

As safety precautions and equipment got better, greater

stretches of time passed before any new dead souls came among us. It was nice to eavesdrop on some living people's conversations. But they mainly talked about the beauty and peacefulness of the mountain. It was a conversation that grew old, and I began to resent it. I saw no beauty or peace on this mountain anymore.

I haven't seen a newly dead soul in over a decade. This was only a guess, of course, since keeping track of time here was difficult. I believe I have been here for around two hundred years now. I am about as old as Alfred was when we first arrived. Of course, he's been here for about four hundred years now. Nothing has changed much in that time. We see new circular-shaped flying craft now, which is interesting.

We have all gotten close. We're like family. However, some of the girls and guys have developed relationships with each other. Most of the girls have slept with most of the guys and vice versa. For that matter, most of the guys have paired up with each other, as have the girls amongst themselves. With so much time and sex being one of our only pleasures, anything and everything possible in that department has been explored. However, sex isn't as pleasurable as it once was. We have no body heat. It is a cold type of love. But it is the best we got.

I haven't heard Juliet mention Adam since our first year of being here. As guilty as I feel about it, I have all but forgotten about Amber. Although, her memory did keep me occupied for the first few decades of my residence here.

I wish I could say I found some answers. Why are we here? What happened to Adam, Ace, and my wife? But none were forthcoming. We just speculated. I've seen no god, angel, demon, or devil. I don't know if this is some sort of punishment or if some dreadful natural law of the universe trapped us here. I suppose if I haven't found out by now, I'll never know.

We talk to each other some, but we've run out of things to talk about over the years. We don't have much of a past and no hope for a future. We mostly sit around and listen to that dreadful sound of silence.

SERIAL HEALER

I have often heard it said that it is a bad sign if someone thinks about death every day. But I wonder how it could be possible to go through a day without thinking about death. Is that not what every moment in your life is headed towards? The end of your story on Earth. How can anyone go through the middle of their story without thinking about the end? I think this culture of wilfully denying our own mortality is much more detrimental to our mental health than thinking about death every day could be.

I never found out where the ability came from. One day my father took my brother and me to see our uncle, who was dying from cancer. I thought about how we were in the last days of being able to see him. We were close. He used to take my brother and me to the lake frequently.

As I hugged him, I felt tingling and warmth come out of my body and flow into him. After that, he got better. They conducted countless tests and found the cancer had gone into complete remission. He lived for several years after. He later told me he remembered hugging me at the hospital, and it had felt like love became a substance that permeated every cell of his body. He said the world had grown bright, like it was producing its own light.

My uncle was also much more energetic after this. He was more active and full of life than he had been before his cancer. Several months after the incident, my uncle took my brother and me hiking. My brother fell off a high ledge and landed on a rock with his back. He couldn't move or feel his legs. My uncle asked me to massage his legs. I did this, and my brother started to feel my hands. Then he started to move his legs. I felt the same tingling and warmth leave me as I had at the hospital. My brother said he felt some kind of "magnetic sensation" just before he started to feel my hands. After this, we hiked back, and my brother had no issues with his back or legs.

My uncle told me he believed I had a gift. He told me my great-grandfather had been a popular faith healer. People from all over testified that he had helped cure them of many ailments. Apparently, further back in our Native American ancestry, we had several medicine men in our family tree.

My uncle started recommending people to me, and my reputation spread through our town and many surrounding towns. I helped so many people in such a short period of time that I quickly became exhausted and drained. I started limiting myself to five people in the mornings and five in the evenings. After a few days of this, I would have to take a week off from seeing people, during which I mostly slept.

Once, I was three days into a week of healing people and had just finished healing the fifth person of the morning, who had had the flu. I was drained and couldn't feel anything anymore. Another person, a young woman, came to me with her child. I was about to tell her I could not heal anymore that day. But she had a pleading look in her eyes that was difficult to say no to. She had heard about me from her cousin who lived here in town. She lived across the country in Rhode Island. Her child had leukaemia, and she had desperately been trying everything to help her child.

I gathered up what was left of my energy into my hands and tried to help her son. When I did this, the sensation was different. I touched him and felt the tingling and warmth flow into me. Instead of feeling drained afterwards, I felt more energetic than I had before I tried to heal the child. The kid was not healed. In fact, he died that very night.

I assumed he was just one of the many I failed to heal. I wasn't always successful. I never knew who I would be able to heal and who I wouldn't. I didn't understand why I could heal some and not others. There seemed to be no rhyme or reason to it.

One day, a man who had a bad reputation around town came to me. I was a friend of his wife and knew he handled her roughly during unjustified fits of anger. He also slept around on her. I didn't like him. He came to me with a high fever and was puking his guts out. It was something minor he could have healed from on his own. It was a virus a couple of his buddies were already recovering from.

However, he wanted immediate relief. I wouldn't have even tried to help him if he hadn't arrived with a couple of his buddies brandishing guns. I reluctantly touched him to heal him. I then experienced the same sensation I had with the child from Rhode Island. I felt the warmth and tingling go from his body into mine. He did not heal immediately. In fact, over the next few hours, it got drastically worse, and he ended up dying.

Someone in their twenties, in fair health, should not have died from such a virus. That was when I began to realize I was responsible. The realization made me feel strangely good. I felt empowered.

A lot of people didn't believe in my power. Because of my many failures. Especially public officials, such as local law enforcement and politicians. At least, these people would never admit to believing in my power, although several have discreetly visited me for their ills.

What about causing these deaths? If I was discreet, no one would ever figure out I could kill people the way I can. I would tell no one. And if anyone suspected, no public official would admit to such a suspicion. It would be too risky for their reputation.

I could learn to control it. I would have power over life and death. I felt very powerful. I started practising my new ability on different people. Once a day, in the late evening, instead of healing a person, I did the other thing. I then found out where they lived or followed them to their homes. I spied on them from outside windows, if it were possible, or sneaked into their homes to watch. I watched as they got worse, as they got sicker. I watched them die.

It was an amazing feeling. Taking someone's life. There is nothing like it. The ecstasy, the thrill, and the feeling of power can only be experienced to be understood. While I enjoyed taking people's lives this way, I knew I had to slow down. So, I started only doing one person every couple of weeks.

Killing with such a large time delay grew less exciting. I wondered if I could take more of this energy, this life force, from people and kill them immediately. Of course, I couldn't do this at one of my healing sessions. Besides, doing this to a healthier specimen would be nice.

I started looking for people in town that would make good targets. I found a twenty-three-year-old blonde woman putting groceries in her car one late evening. I watched from my car in the parking lot. I followed as she got in her car and drove home.

I waited for her to finish unloading her groceries then I walked up to the front door of her house. As I approached her door, I got so excited my heart raced. It was a mixture of nervousness and excitement. I knocked on the door. She answered. I was shaking at first, but I quickly put my left hand over her mouth and pushed her against the wall just inside the house. I grabbed her left hand in my right hand.

Her eyes were wide with terror. She struggled to break free from my grip. She grew weaker. I watched as her eyes started to relax and gradually become emotionless. I watched as the life drained from her. I loosened my hold, and she fell limply to the ground. Her body made a loud thump on hitting the floor.

When this happened, I was startled to hear a loud male voice coming from the living room.

"Is everything ok?" he called.

My heart raced. I did not anticipate this. There was someone else here. He walked in and looked at the girl on the ground. He then looked at me with an expression of surprise and shock.

I quickly put my hand over his chest and pushed him into the house. He pushed me back, tackling me to the door. I continued to touch his wrist as his hands strangled my neck.

"What did you do?" he yelled at me.

His grip loosened, growing weaker as I drained him. He finally fell to the ground. His eyes shut, and his skin pale. He had no pulse. He was gone.

I quickly left the house. I looked around as I walked out, making sure there were no witnesses. I got in my car and drove off.

The next evening I watched the local news. After the woman didn't show up for work, a friend tried to call her. She hadn't responded for hours, so her friend went to check on her. She found her and her boyfriend dead.

Her name was Jane Pepper. She was a local elementary school teacher. Her boyfriend was Brian Baker. He worked at a used tire shop. They met when she needed a flat tire repaired. I learned this from her friend as she told the story to the news reporter on TV.

Knowing this information about the couple, making me feel as if I knew personal things about them, added a different dimension to my killing. I watched as her friend on the news cried. It made me realize I had changed so many lives. Not just the couple that I killed but also their friends and family. All their loved ones. When I healed, I pretty much always returned people's lives back to normal, back to what it was like before they got ill. Real change only happened if they had been blind or paralyzed for years or something like that. These situations were rare, however. Anyway, killing was much more thrilling for some reason.

These people's lives would change and never be the same. I smiled. It made me feel somewhat like a god.

I had to be more careful with my next prey. I found a young female brunette with a small frame. I stalked her for days. She did have a boyfriend, but he didn't live with her. He was only at her house on weekend nights, Friday through Sunday. On weekday nights, she was alone. She also lived in a rural area. I learned she worked as a cashier at the dollar store. Her name was Tracy.

After doing my homework, I decided on the night of the kill. I waited until her lights went out and she had gone to bed. I took a crowbar to the back door furthest from her room. It made a louder noise than I anticipated. I stopped and waited silently, listening for signs that I had startled her. I heard nothing, so I made my way to her bedroom.

When I looked in her bedroom, her eyes were wide open and staring. She had been listening. She must have heard me but was too scared to do anything. She had a deer-in-the-headlights look.

I approached her, and she kept staring at me. Her

breathing grew more rapid. She finally managed to ask, "What do you want?"

I gently put my hand on her forehead and slowly rubbed it across her face.

"Are you going to rape me?" she asked.

"No," I said. "I want to watch you die as I kill you."

She whimpered, "Why?"

"Because I can," I replied.

She started to cry but quickly grew quiet as I drained the life out of her. After she fell completely silent, I decided I would hide her body. No one would be able to figure out what happened to my victims for now. I was killing them in a way no one understood. I wasn't even sure I really understood it. But I didn't want them to eventually figure it out if I just left the bodies lying around.

There was a lake nearby that I had planned to dump the body in. There was a canoe that someone near the lake left tied up on the shore. I took the plastic garbage bag containing her body, a rope, and cement blocks. I rowed to the lake's centre, tied the bag to the cement blocks, and dumped it overboard. I then rowed the boat back and tied it up.

A couple of days later, I saw her boyfriend on the news, saying he couldn't get a hold of her and she wasn't at her house. No one knew where she was. She was a missing person. They pleaded with everyone through the television set for any information that could lead the police to find her. They offered a reward.

There was another unique and empowering feeling in being the only one who knew where she was. Being the only one who knew for a fact that she was dead and their hope and pleas were in vain. I was the only one who knew what happened to my victims. It was like being the only one who knew a secret. I was tempted to let someone in on the secret so they knew that I knew. So they knew what I did, what I could do, what I could get away with. Of course, that was not possible. It gave me a sense of closeness to my victims to know we were the only ones who knew what happened. Like I own a piece of their soul. Now you, too, are in on the secret, dear reader.

I have continued with this hobby of mine. I have killed thirteen girls in the past couple of years. I still do my healing sessions. I can heal more people during my sessions now. I don't know if it's the thrill of the killing or the life force I take from my victims that help me do more healing, maybe both. I feel more invigorated now. After I kill, a greater percentage of my healings are successful.

How do I justify it? Well, my kills help me heal more people. Also, I contribute all this life to my community. Do I not deserve to take some life in return?

THE NIGHTMARE

Dreams. What are they? Are they random firings in the brain? Where do they come from? Where do they originate? Are they messages from the subconscious or the spirit realm? I have had some strange dreams. I have had some frightening nightmares. But none have ever been as strange or terrifying as the one I had on this particular night.

It was April 1873. I reread the letter in my hand as I sat on the train, scenery flitting by my window. I wore my business attire, a gray suit pants and gray overtop jacket. My fedora lay beside me on my seat. I listened to the noise of the train as the steam engine drove it across the tracks. I was heading to a small town called Fairplay near the eastern shore of Georgia.

The letter was written to me about a haunting:

Dear Mr. Huntington,

We have something in our house keeping us up at night. We have seen apparitions. We have had our dishes fly across the room and break against the wall. We are unable to sleep at night because of the fear and noise caused by these incidents. These phenomena have been witnessed not just by my wife and I but also by a constable and our priest. Our priest tried to perform an exorcism but to no effect. Please, perhaps your expertise in this area could be of benefit to us.

Sincerely,
Tom Campbell

I had investigated a few hauntings and poltergeists throughout the country as well as in Europe. I have attempted to stop these hauntings in the past, but nothing seemed to work. Usually, when something did appear to work, the phenomena had already become weaker and were probably at the end of running their course like they eventually did. It is equivalent to taking some snake oil when you're sick but about to get better anyway, then crediting the snake oil when you do get better.

However, this case sounded interesting, although typical of others I had encountered. The train stopped near Fairplay at 8:00 p.m. It was late, and I was tired from the long journey, so I decided to find lodging for the night. Being such a small area, finding a vacant room at a local inn proved no difficulty.

I actually recall reading about this town a couple of times in the Society for Psychical Research's periodicals. It was a publication that compiled reports of their investigations. This town seemed to have abnormally high amounts of strange hauntings compared to most places. Perhaps this was some kind of local folklore that had developed, or maybe there was something about this place.

There was a river next to the inn I stayed in. I took a walk along its banks since I enjoy the relaxation of a running river under a clear starry night sky. There were a lot of stones on the riverbed, and the currents ran rapidly over them. A few large granite rocks came stuck on the side of the river. They were covered in quartz veins that disappeared into the river and shimmered in the moonlight.

I finished enjoying my walk and decided to head back to my room. I planned on meeting the Campbells fairly early in the morning. It was very quiet in my room. I am unsure if the inn hosted any other guests that night. I blew out the candles and lay in my bed. The room gave off an eerie ambience in the darkness and silence.

I woke up in my bed suddenly, unable to move. At first, it was a curious sensation, but it quickly became terrifying. I tried to move a finger, turn my head, or wiggle a toe. I was all to no avail. I could turn my eyes to look in any direction, but that was it.

I started to feel a vibration throughout my body. At first, the sensation was subtle, but then the vibration became more intense. I heard a humming sound that grew louder as the vibration intensified. I felt myself becoming lighter and started floating out of my bed. I was levitating. I was finally able to open my eyes. When I did, the ceiling was pressing right up against me.

I was able to move now, and so I turned over to look down. There seemed to be a person lying on my bed beneath me. On closer inspection, I realized the person looked just like me. It was me! There was a cord of shimmering silver light connecting the me on the ceiling to the me on the bed.

I turned back around towards the ceiling and placed my hand on it. I felt the rough texture of the ceiling beneath my palm. I pushed my hand harder against the ceiling, and it went right through. I could feel the structures inside the ceiling and inside the roof. Then my hand met the cool night air as my arm stretched all the way through the top of the roof.

I willed myself to float up and glided through the roof and into the clear night sky. I continued to float up. I felt incredibly free. It seemed The body in my bed felt like a prison in comparison. It just slowed and weighed me down. Now I was free from that sack of flesh, and it left me ecstatic.

I flew higher into the sky and looked toward the ground. I saw the town below me getting smaller. As I flew up higher, I felt rapid vibrations come over me. The higher I got, the faster the vibrations became and the more ecstatic I got.

The cord between the real me and the me in my room kept stretching. It looked much thinner than it had earlier. In fact, I felt it tugging.

I flew back to the room. Hovering above the me in the bed, above my body, was a swirling spiral of darkness. It looked almost like a void in space. It was messing with the cord connecting to my body. It seemed to be trying to break it. Would I die if it was successful? Would it take my body? While I enjoyed this state I was in, I did not want to die.

Terror welled up inside me. I flew to my body to try and reenter it. The dark swirling thing moved between me and my body, then it chased after me. I flew out above the roof, and it followed me out. It got the part of the cord that was closer to me and started to attack it again.

I flew over and tried to kick it. As I did, I felt my foot being sucked into it, warping and tearing apart. I recoiled and flew away. The leg that I kicked with was gone. I hurried back towards my room and body, turned over, and lay parallel to my body. I floated to line back up with it. As I did this, I saw the dark spiraling rushing through the ceiling towards me. It was about to reach me when I opened my eyes and woke up.

I was in my body, or maybe I had woken up from a dream. I was not sure. I got out of bed and immediately plopped down on the floor. I had no feeling in my right leg. I could barely get it to move. It was the same leg I had kicked the creature with in my vision.

I did not sleep the rest of that night. The next day, I got an employee from the inn to help me to the pharmacy, where I bought a cane. A doctor nearby tested the leg with the standard pinpricks and reflexes. The leg reacted to nothing. The doctor said it seemed there was no activity in my nervous system in that leg. It was pretty much dead. Blood circulation was poor. It was paler than the rest of my body and cold to the touch.

I was told to watch for any cuts or abrasions on the leg as it was probably too weak to heal or fight against infections. This can lead to more complications. The doctor had no idea what caused the mysterious condition.

The doctor suggested amputation to avoid possible life-threatening conditions in the future. I would then be given a prosthetic leg made of wood. I went along with the doctor's suggestion.

After recovering from the procedure, I took the train back home to San Francisco. I wrote a letter to Mr. Campbell apologizing for my absence. I just wanted to get out of town and have nothing to do with spirits again.

I do not know if some being of swirling darkness had stolen the life out of my leg, if I had had a dream telling me something was wrong with my leg, or if it were a prophetic dream of me losing my leg. The vision was so real. Either way, it was a strange coincidence.

WRITER'S BLOCK

West was a large man. He always wore a baseball cap and sported a wide beard. He was the type of man who focused on his work until he got it done. He had made quite a name for himself as a writer. He had written eleven novels so far and had signed a contract for a twelfth. The problem was he had developed that infamous disability, writer's block.

He had built quite a life from the money he made off his past novels. But he needed another novel to sustain his lifestyle. He had a mortgage on an expensive house and a beautiful wife who loved him for his success and money more than anything else. She was a person who liked to lay back for most of the day and watch crime documentaries or keep up with the news on the serial killer that had been killing across the southeast.

West sat at an old Irish pub called Mullens in the downtown area of Seneca, South Carolina. It was where he came to think, especially when he was feeling down. He was drinking Bud Light and listening to the drunks attempt to sing on the karaoke machine while people danced to the music.

An older man sat beside him. He looked like life had weathered him over the years. His face was rough and full of wrinkles. He had some teeth missing. One eye opened and was expressive, but the other did not change along with the rest of his face. In all the times West had come to this bar, he did not recall ever seeing him.

"You're that writer, ain't ya?" the man asked West in a hoarse voice.

"Yes," West replied. Although he didn't feel much like talking. West found it odd that the man would recognize him. He didn't look like a man who would be into the romance novels West wrote. He looked more like a man who, if he did read, would be into war novels.

"When you coming out with your next book?" he asked.

"I'm working on it. Just trying to come up with an idea."

West wouldn't normally add that last part, especially when talking to a stranger. Maybe the alcohol has gotten him in a more open mood than usual.

"That's a shame. I always look forward to them. I'm retired, and I ain't got no one. It's one of the few things that keep me from killing myself out of boredom," he said.

The stranger sipped at his drink for a bit before continuing.

"I got something that might help you," he said, pulling out a small figurine from his pocket. It was made of weathered stone. It looked like a person belonging to a nomadic tribe in the desert. It wore a desert hood and scarf that people used to cover and protect their faces from sandstorms. It was almost impossible to make out detailed features. These seem to have disappeared over time.

"Someone gave this to me when I was overseas in the desert. I was young at the time and had a band. We had dreams, but it was more of a hobby, and we all settled into average lives. Anyway, the man told me it would help me come up with magnificent songs. I was told to sleep with it under my pillow. I tried it and woke up with whole songs in my head. The music and lyrics and everything."

West thought that sounded ridiculous, but he was willing to try anything right now. He took it and thanked the stranger.

"One more thing," the man added cryptically. "When you take something from it, you have to give something back. It is like an exchange."

He brought up his left hand to show West. Half of his index finger was missing.

"After I played the first song, I lost my finger in a lawn mower accident. The motor was off. I reached down to check the blade, and the motor suddenly ran. The blades spun and caught my finger. After I played the second song, my wife of twelve years divorced me. This was unexpected and sudden. I thought we were doing good, but it turned out she had found someone better. My friends said I was becoming superstitious, blaming it on that thing you have in your hand. I decided not to take any chances and stopped using it. But it may be worth it for a big-time writer like you."

West thanked the man again, finished his beer, and walked back home. When he got home, he threw the thing under his pillow and went to sleep. That night he dreamed about two ex-lovers who found each other and rekindled their love despite both already being remarried. The dream was detailed and memorable. It was a great story. When West woke up, he found a notebook and wrote down the dream.

He was able to write the novel in just a few days based on the dream. It was an immediate success. He didn't really give credit to the gift the strange man had given to him at the bar.

He had been thinking about the novel for a while. Perhaps his subconscious finally caved and gave him something in a dream, or perhaps the figurine acted as a confidence booster.

Not long after his book was published, he woke up with blurry vision in his left eye. He thought nothing of it and figured it would go away. But as the day went on, he completely lost vision in that eye. He called the doctor, who recommended he go to the hospital. It turned out he had an eye stroke. A blood clot had interrupted blood flow to the eye. By the time he got to the hospital, it was too late, and he had permanently lost vision in that eye.

Time passed, and he landed a contract for a thirteenth book. He tried to come up with something for a new story, but he had hit another writer's block. Perhaps he was all out of ideas. Maybe the books he had already written were the only ideas his brain could come up with. He thought about the figurine again. He put it under his pillow again and went to sleep. He dreamed of another great idea for a story. He woke up and immediately wrote it down.

Once again, the book got published and was a huge success. One day he went to a book signing at a local bookstore. When he came home, his house was ablaze. He called 911, and they came to put out the fire. But it was too late. All that was left was the foundation, a pile of debris, and half a wall still standing.

West and his wife decided to rent a small place until they could get something better. West began to wonder if there was something to what the stranger in the bar had said. Maybe he shouldn't use the figurine anymore. He threw it in the back of his closet. He wasn't sure the figurine had anything to do with his success and bad luck, but he'd rather be safe.

He needed to write something new so he could afford to buy a house as nice, if not nicer, than the one that burned down. West's wife was growing ever dissatisfied with their current situation. He didn't want her to lose interest.

He tried and tried to come up with a new idea. He tried for months and couldn't come up with any ideas at all, good or bad. The thought of using the figurine kept crossing his mind. The thoughts came more frequently the more time passed, and no ideas presented themselves. West went to his closet, dug around in the back, and found the figurine. He put it under his pillow and went to sleep.

Once again, he woke up dreaming of a perfect romantic story. He wrote the novel, and it became a huge success. He was able to buy a nice huge house. His wife was happy again, and so was he.

On his way home one day, he got a call from the police department. His wife had been found dead. Somebody had dropped off her body onto the side of Interstate 85. It was the M.O. of the serial killer his wife had been watching on the news. Apparently, he had been dropping bodies off the sides of interstates across the southeast of the United States. The FBI had been searching for him for a while.

West was devastated. He screamed out in grief when he got the call. He fell into a depression. He started drinking a case of beer every night. He would drink until he passed out. It was the only way he could go to sleep. Otherwise, his thoughts would torment him late into the night. He couldn't make them stop. He swore he would never use the figurine again. A deep hatred for it grew inside of him. He wanted it destroyed. So he lit his fireplace and threw it inside. He sat in front of the fire regretting ever accepting the cursed object.

He thought about the man who gave him the thing. He had never seen him in that bar before that night. He had been there a few times since and hadn't seen him again either. What are the chances that the one time he met the guy, he was at his most vulnerable? The most likely time for him to make a deal with the devil. Is that who the man was? The devil? He was certainly no angel.

As time passed, he continued to drink his health and wealth away. It got to the point once again where he couldn't pay for the mortgage or his nightly habits. He wasn't sure if he cared about keeping the house anymore, but he certainly didn't want to be homeless.

He decided to write another book. One more, so he could continue his lifestyle a little longer. He tried and tried but could not come up with any good ideas.

He thought about the figurine. He had destroyed it though. A good thing because if he hadn't, he might have been tempted to use it again. "Maybe…" he thought. The figurine was made of some kind of stone. It couldn't truly be destroyed in the fire.

He dug through the ashes for the first time since he threw the thing in. There, deeply buried in the ashes, was a stone piece. You couldn't make out any of the details on the stone anymore, but surely it would still work.

Did he dare use it again? Just one more time, then he would stop. After all, he had nothing else to lose. All that mattered to him had already been taken away.

He slowly put the burned figurine under his pillow that night. He drank until he passed out on the bed. That night he dreamed of a story of a woman unknowingly in love with a serial killer. He wrote the book, and it got published. It went to the top of the best sellers list.

West's health started to deteriorate. He forgot things, repeating things he had said just a few minutes before. The doctors told him alcohol severely damaged his liver and told him to slow down his drinking. West did not listen. Soon too many toxins built up in his liver, and he became disorientated and unable to get out of his bed. He did not really have any friends or family that he kept in regular contact with, so no one came to check on him for a couple of weeks. The publisher had been trying to get a hold of him for a book signing event. After not reaching through to him for several days, the publisher went to his house to check on him.

The front door was unlocked, so he went in and found West dead in his bed. Beside the bed, on the floor, he found a stone figurine. It looked like it was wearing a baseball cap and had a wide beard.

The publisher dialled a number on his phone. "We have milked everything we could out of this one. I have another client that needs some inspiration if you can make the delivery.

"Of course," a hoarse voice said on the other end. It was a strange man that delivered the figurine. He had a lazy right eye, and half of his left index finger was missing.

THE GODS ARE COMING

Aaron was picking blackberries on the edge of the woods by a pond. The pond lay deep in the woods. It was a quiet place. It's where he came to think and get away from the noise of his family. It was a beautiful summer morning in the mountains of western North Carolina. It was a morning on which you would expect nothing to happen. Nothing bad, anyway. Aaron should have known better. He was a news anchor and was used to presenting news of horrible things that happened on perfect days. Things like school shootings, fatal car wrecks, and mysterious disappearances.

As he finished picking blackberries, he turned towards the pond and saw a silvery cylinder-shaped object floating several yards above it. It was utterly silent and floated at a complete standstill. Suddenly a bright light beamed from it directly at Aaron. He was disoriented as it felt like all his weight had left him. He felt light as a feather. It seemed the Earth had ceased pulling at him. Instead, his body felt attracted to and pulled toward the object. As he moved closer to the object, he blacked out.

ON THE BORDERS OF REALITY

He awoke in an empty metallic room. He lay in the middle of the room on a table made from the same metal. Aaron was dazed. He wasn't sure if he was in a dream or if this was reality. The room did not seem to have any doors or windows. It looked like a solid continuous wall. Was this some high-tech casket? Suddenly an extremely tall being emerged right through the wall like a ghost. Aaron estimated the being was about nine feet tall. It looked human, although there was no hair on its head. It also had abnormally large eyes. The being communicated with him through a series of thoughts and images in his mind. At first, it projected pure emotion at Aaron, causing him to feel instantly calm and numb. He could tell the thoughts and feelings were not coming from him but from outside his mind.

The being explained that he wanted Aaron to act as a messenger. They chose him for his access to a wide audience in such a powerful country. The message was that the gods had returned, and humans needed to prepare by gathering offerings and building altars.

Aaron responded, "Why not tell the governments this? I have no power to tell humans what to do."

He was not sure if the being would understand him when he spoke in English and hoped it would understand the thoughts behind his words. The being told him they had no need for human authority to tell humans what to do. He said they were the new authority. They just needed a way to get the message out.

Aaron asked the being who and what they were. If he had to tell people the gods had returned, he would like to know who these "gods" were. The being seemed to take offense at this remark but proceeded to explain through a series of thoughts and images.

They came from a world that circled our star at a great distance. The planet was massive, and its core created enough heat for life to survive on the surface. The planet's orbit never got too close to our star. They developed technology that enabled them to reach us when their planet was a certain distance from the Earth. Every five thousand Earth years, the planet comes within contact distance. Then they were close enough to our planet to maintain continual contact for one thousand years. When the planet approached the Earth, its intense gravity caused earthquakes, floods, and major climate change. It seemed apocalyptic to humans.

When they first found our planet, it was full of primitive life forms. Primitive mammals, birds, and reptiles. They were masters of genetic engineering and wanted to make slaves from some of these creatures as they had from primitive life forms on their planet. They experimented with different reptiles, fish, mammals, and birds. The experiments led to many of the different creatures man has found and recorded in fossil records, thinking they were just ancient animals. Some of their offspring even survived in our myths and legends.

The final decision came down to mammals and birds. While they were both potentially very intelligent, it was decided that mammal minds were far easier to control than rebellious bird minds. They needed a creature from among the mammals that not only possessed both traits, intelligence and servitude, but also had bodies capable of moving around while grasping things and manipulating tools. So they meddled with genetic engineering, leaving certain mammals to develop this way.

When they came back, they found different levels of success. Apes and monkeys had developed, as well as various humanoids. The homo sapiens were smarter than most of the others, excluding what humans later called the Neanderthals. The Neanderthals were rebellious, however. The gods decided to wipe all humanoid species out except the homo sapiens since humans were good at working in groups and were the perfect servants.

In their next round, they had humans create monuments to them. Humans were too small for some tasks, so they altered human DNA again and made what they called Nephilites. These were the giants recorded in humanity's ancient legends. They helped move stones to build the pyramids.

The gods taught man agriculture and other sciences that helped them master the craft, such as astronomy, working with fire, and primitive chemistry. They taught them law systems as laid down by them and the invention of monetary systems. All these teachings were meant to ensure that many people could live in one area without having to constantly move about.

Some of the giants left with the aliens to serve them. The rest were killed by ancient warriors. The being standing before Aaron was one of them. This is why he looked so similar to a human. These giants were unable to reproduce but the ones that went with the aliens were kept alive indefinitely through alien technology. This one standing before Aaron had grown up in ancient Egypt.

The Aliens themselves had life spans that were much longer than humans. Living on average for between 9000-10000 years. They reproduced only once in a lifetime. So many of the "gods" of ancient Egypt, and in the myths of the surrounding areas like Babylon, Greece, and Rome, were still alive. And they were soon to arrive on Earth.

Because they lived such long lives, these beings developed and mostly lived with older minds. Fresh ideas were rare, and they did not work well in groups. As a result, their technology had not developed much. Still, they had developed new drone spacecraft that could reach the Earth before their planet was close enough to transport themselves back and forth between the planets. People have been seeing these "UFOs" for the past century or so.

The aliens' bodies consisted of a gaseous plasma. When their metabolisms are in overdrive, they can appear almost invisible to humans by producing light at a high-frequency range. Normally, they appeared as bright light to humans. However, their powerful telepathic abilities could make weak-minded humans believe they looked like all sorts of things.

Aaron was privileged to be shown all of this information because he had been chosen as a messenger.

"What do the aliens call themselves?" Aaron asked.

"Gods," the giant said. "That is what they are. Amon is in command. He is king of the gods, the god of gods. I am Imhotep, the god Thoth's right-hand man. I lead the building of the pyramids."

"Catastrophes will happen as our planet approaches yours. Volcanoes will erupt. The weather will become chaotic. When we are close enough to arrive, we will save you from the devastation," the giant said.

"Are you not here now?" Aaron asked, confused.

Imhotep communicated that they were standing in a drone, and the room was built to enhance his telepathic projection. This is what Aaron was looking at.

"Announce on the television that we are coming," Imhotep said as Aaron became dizzy and passed out.

Aaron woke up in his bed. At first, he wondered if his experience had been a dream. However, the skin on his chest was painfully sensitive. When he took his shirt to look at it, he saw that his skin had been burned. He rushed to the hospital, and they said he had somehow suffered radiation burns.

He didn't know what these aliens expected. If he announced "the gods are coming" on the news, no one would believe him. He would lose his job and be sent away for psychiatric treatment. He decided to report his experience to the Navy, who had a protocol for reporting such things. He told them natural disasters were on the way. Perhaps the humans could fight back.

He also called FEMA to warn them, saying he knew they wouldn't believe him, but they should be on the lookout. He also used his connections to get the word to some high-ranking generals in the army and air force. Surprisingly, a few days later, a couple of men in suits showed up at his door. They said they worked for a special department within the government and asked Aaron to report his entire experience again.

Of course, nothing came of this. At least, it didn't seem so. There were no signs the government was raising defences or preparing for an interspatial battle. Eight months later, a news anchor on the Fox channel started saying crazy things about aliens coming to the planet. Needless to say, nobody ever saw him on television again.

Two years passed, and then earthquakes hit California, Japan, and India at practically the same time. The earthquakes were devastating, like nothing the world had ever seen. Volcanoes erupted in several parts of the world, including Yellowstone National Park. More hurricanes hit the southeastern United States that year than any other year. There were floods in the Amazon, tsunamis in China, and freezing blizzards in northern Europe that froze their water pipes and took their power out.

Many thought the end of the world was happening. Apocalyptic cults and groups of religious fanatics popped up everywhere. Churches had more visitors than they had had for decades. Soon spacecraft were seen in the sky. They were massive and like nothing the world had seen before. The ships were diamond-shaped.

When the ships landed, they melted the ground beneath them, softening it enough for the bottom half of the diamond to sink firmly and provide a stable foundation. The upper half of the diamond stayed above ground. Because of this, the ships looked like pyramids when they landed.

Aaron was at home when he heard banging outside. He received a telepathic message telling him to come outside. Aaron was frightened but could not make himself disobey the telepathic command. He came out of his house and found Imhotep.

"You did not deliver the message," he communicated to Aaron.

"I am sorry, no one would believe…"

Imhotep snatched Aaron's head with one hand, lifting him off the ground. Aaron felt the pressure increasing around his head. The pressure turned into unbearable pain until Aaron couldn't feel anything anymore. His body fell to the ground. His skull was no longer identifiable as a skull.

The government had a secret program preparing for this eventuality. The information they gleaned from UFO and alien contact reports had, in fact, been taken seriously in case they turned out to be a national threat. The United States contacted governments from other powerful nations to work out strategies. The aliens themselves possessed primitive armour and weapons. Weapons akin to crossbows with the capability of producing intense heat that could burn infrastructures. They discovered the aliens could easily be shot and killed. From what they studied of the spacecraft, it seemed nuclear weapons would be able to take them out.

Since the craft contained most of the aliens' advanced tech, strategies focused around taking them out first. This would also kill most of the aliens at one time. The countries carefully coordinated and shot their nuclear weapons at the same time for a surprise attack. The plan of attack was decided quickly to avoid the risk of the aliens discovering it. Surprise was humanity's greatest ally.

Most of the aliens were destroyed by the nuclear attack, as was much of Earth's environment. After this, a protracted war ensued. It was the worst war the Earth had ever seen. While the aliens had primitive armour and weapons, they quickly learned to use earthling weapons. The Nephilites were incredibly strong and fast, and it took many earthlings to bring them down. The aliens had powerful telepathic abilities, but their bodies were weak and could be destroyed using laser technology and magnetic fields that slowed down their molecules. Technology developed rapidly in the early 21st century.

After the craft were destroyed, the few remaining aliens were severely outnumbered. The earthlings came together and worked in groups, following their military leaders. This structure helped them develop strategies to take the aliens down. Many proudly gave their lives to save the Earth and their fellow humans.

Some aliens managed to escape underground, hiding in the bottom sections of the craft that were buried in the ground. These had functioned as nuclear blast bunkers. But eventually, they were killed as well. After the war, the earthling population was a fraction of what it had been before the war. But they had won. They won because of their predisposition to serve each other, sacrifice their lives for each other, work in groups, and follow leadership. They won because their lifespans were shorter than the aliens'. Humanity reproduced faster, so society was always filled with fresh minds and fresh ideas. The mortals won because of their mortality and willingness to serve a greater cause. Mankind had finally risen up and freed itself from the gods. The gods were dead, man had killed them.

THE THIEF TRAP

Tom looked through the window at a solid gold statue of a ship sitting on a shelf of the family's entertainment centre below the television. The window was open just enough to see it. The family living in the house had not been in the neighbourhood for long. They only moved in a few months ago. They must not have heard about the string of robberies in the area. Tom, Brad, and Richard had been casing out the family's house for a couple of weeks.

Tom and his friends didn't have anything to do with the other robberies that had been happening in the area. Only a few houses had been hit. They were, however, inspired by them. The area was full of reasonably wealthy families. People like doctors, lawyers, and company CEOs were common in this type of neighbourhood. The houses were nice and most had security systems. The thieves who had been hitting the houses grabbed as much as they could in just a few minutes and then ran before they could get caught.

This house did not seem to have a security system. Tom acted like he was making a pizza delivery to the wrong place to look at what he could see inside. He did not see a keypad or anything. He did not see anything through the windows of the house either. There wasn't a sign out front informing you that some security company protected the house. These people must be extremely naive and comfortable. They would be easy targets.

Tom didn't want to just break in and take what he could as quickly as possible. He didn't want this to be a career. He just wanted to hit one time to get what he needed. All he wanted was enough money to get him through until he could find another job. The plant he was working at had shut down and put a lot of people out of work. The job market was flooded, and opportunities became few and far between. He needed to pay rent, groceries, and his daughter's insulin, which was very expensive without medical insurance.

Keith and Brad also worked at the plant. Keith needed money to take care of his wife and eight-month-old son. Brad didn't have anyone he was taking care of. He was only nineteen years old. He said his parent wouldn't let him live in the house, though. Tom wasn't sure how much of that was true. He suspected Brad just wanted the thrill.

The plan was to wear masks and take Mr. Holbrooks' wife and kids hostage. He would then make Mr. Holbrooks go to the bank ATM and withdraw sixty grand from his savings. This would give each of them twenty grand, which should be plenty until they found other jobs. Brad wanted more and argued with him at first, but he finally agreed to only take the sixty thousand. He would, however, take a couple of things from the house, including that gold ship, to supplement his takings. Tom had opened a bank statement he found in the Holbrook mailbox and saw the guy had almost two hundred grand in his savings.

They had been casing out the place for a couple of weeks to observe the family's living pattern, like when everyone went to bed. The kids were older and would sometimes stay up until almost midnight. The adults usually went to bed around ten. Tom, Keith, and Brad snuck in through the back door on an overcast night. Keith picked the lock. He had been picking locks since he was seventeen years old. It was a strange hobby but turned out to be a useful skill every once in a while, such as at this moment.

After a few minutes, Keith got the door opened. They snuck into the house quietly. They were careful to look for any security traps they could not see from the outside. A strange cable was embedded in the carpet not too far from the back door. It seemed to go around the perimeter of the living room. They didn't think anything of it. They used flashlights with red lens coverings to look around the house. They wore knitted thermal masks to hide their faces and black rubber gloves. Brad carried a sawed-off shotgun, and Tom and Keith each carried a 9mm Glock fixed with silencers. Tom told Brad not to bring the shotgun because it would be too loud. He said it was only for intimidation, just like Tom and Keith's guns were. He wasn't going to use his, just like they had no plan of using theirs. Of course, if things went bad enough, they would do what they had to do.

Brad took the girl's room, Keith took the boy's room, and Tom took Andrew Holbrook and his wife's room. Tom walked in and saw the wife on the left side of the bed. He put his left hand over the wife's mouth and the gun up to her head with his right hand. Taylor reached her hand over and grabbed Andrew's wrist. Andrew opened his eyes.

"Be quiet, or I will put a bullet in her head," Tom said.

Andrew's eyes grew wide with shock and fear.

"You are going to go to the living room, and I will follow you," Tom commanded.

Andrew got up and went to the living room. Brad and Keith already had the kids there, seventeen-year-old Selma and twelve-year-old Carter. They carried three kitchen chairs and placed them in the living room. Keith made Selma tie up her brother, and Tom made Andrew tie up Taylor. Brad tied up Selma.

"Ooh, you pulled that tight," she said, trying to put a seductive smile on her face.

"Okay, Andrew, we will go upstairs to get you dressed."

They went upstairs, and Tom watched Andrew carefully as he put on his clothes. They went back down to the living room.

"Okay, this is what is going to happen. Mr. Holbrooks and I are going to go to the bank, where he will withdraw sixty thousand dollars for us. You guys are going to stay here. If Andrew tries to do anything I don't tell him to do, I will call my buddies here, and they will shoot one of you. I will leave it up to their discretion. But as long as everyone remains cooperative, there will be no issues. We will get our money, we will leave, and you people can return to your normal lives like nothing ever happened. Understood?" They all nodded in agreement.

Tom and Andrew left the house. Brad sat down in a chair, holding the shotgun so it stayed aimed at the family. Keith looked down in shame.,

"You know this isn't something I would normally do. I just need money right now," he said, breaking the silence.

"You don't have to explain yourself," Brad said. "In fact, it is probably better if you don't. Me? I like doing this. It's exciting. I can't explain why."

Selma spoke up, "It's to escape the robot."

"What?" Brad asked, confused.

"The reason this is exciting, doing crime is exciting, is to escape the robot," Selma continued. "The robot is an idea the author Colin Wilson came up with. He said a robot lives in each of us. It takes over all automated tasks. Meaning anything you do routinely that eventually becomes a habit. The robot can take over when you're driving a route you drive every day. That's why you look back and don't even remember driving. The robot takes over all kinds of things. When you go to the same job every day, it takes over. Whether it's coming home and eating dinner, or engaging in some recreational activity you've done for a long time, such as going to a bar, hunting, or playing ball. After a while, the robot takes over all of this too. If these things are all that your life consists of, then the robot will take over your life."

She paused to see if anyone would interrupt her and continued when no one said anything. "When the robot takes over, you become disconnected from life. You begin to live life from behind a film or through tinted glass. You're not living life fully. So people do things that break them out of the routine if they can and if they aren't too scared. They do things like cheat, rob, and cause drama—anything that would break them out of their routine. They try to escape the robot so they can reconnect with life. That is all you're doing, trying to feel alive." Her eyes glazed over, and her voice grew solemn as she said all this.

"I have never heard it put in such a poetic way before," Brad said. "I like it."

Selma looked at Brad. She narrowed her eyes, licked her lips, and said, "You know, you don't have to keep aiming that gun toward me...We could..." She looked him up and down and continued, "Have some fun." She batted her eyebrows at him.

"Oh, yeah? Just how old are you?" Brad asked

"I'm seventeen, legal in this state," Selma asked.

"No! Young lady, you will not do that. You need to wait until you're eighteen," Taylor protested.

Selma rolled her eyes. "You see what I mean? I know all about trying to escape the robot."

Brad looked at Keith. Keith shook his head, and Brad sighed, saying, "Looks like we both got people trying to tell us what to do. I am going to take you up on some fun anyway. It's a good way to kill time while we wait here."

So Brad untied her, and they went up to her room.

"Do you like to roleplay?" Selma asked Brad as they made their way up.

"Sure," Brad answered.

"I want to roleplay like you're the big bad robber, and you have come to take me and force me to do your bidding. I will cry, fight a little, and pretend I don't like it. It is a fantasy of mine," Selma said.

"Sure," Brad said. "I like it a little rough."

Brad pulled the covers up on the bed. Selma quickly switched on her laptop camera while he was turned away. She got on the bed. Brad got on top of her, and she pushed at him. He pushed back and roughly pulled her pants down. She looked at the camera with a grimace on her face and started to cry quietly.

Downstairs, Keith went to the bathroom. When he came back, he saw Carter's chair was empty. It looked like the rope had been cut.

"Shit," he said in a near panic. "Where did he go?"

Taylor looked over to her right. Keith looked and saw the door to the basement was open. He went to the door.

"Where are you, boy? Come back up here." He heard no response.

Keith started to make his way down the stairs. All of a sudden, he felt a sharp pain on the back of his foot. He lost all strength in that foot and toppled down the stairs. Something had cut his Achilles tendon. Carter stood over him, holding a knife.

Keith grabbed at him, but Carter dodged and ran deeper into the basement. Keith stood up in pain, limped forward a step, and leapt at Carter. As he leapt, he felt a force come down hard on his back, knocking him down to the ground.

Keith looked up to see Taylor standing there holding a baseball bat. Carter grabbed Keith's gun from its holster while he was still getting his bearings. He pointed it at Keith.

"There is a chair over there," he said, pointing to a chair in the corner of the basement.

"Get in it," Taylor ordered him.

Keith crawled to the chair. It had metal wrist restraints on the arms and ankle restraints on the front legs. He clambered into the chair, and Taylor snapped the restraints around his wrists and ankles. Mother and son both smiled at each other.

"I think that when you hit him with a baseball bat in self-defence, you could have broken his jaw," Carter said.

"Yes, if he turned his head to look after I hit him in the back and I was frightened in the moment, I could see me hitting him in the face," Taylor said.

She brought the bat up high over her shoulder and swung it, striking the right side of Keith's face. The impact rocked his head back, sending a sharp pain shooting through his face. The right side of his vision blurred. He could barely see out of that eye.

Taylor and Carter laughed almost psychotically. It seemed they were actually having fun. Taylor took a claw hammer off a table nearby. She swung it as hard as she could on Keith's right hand. A sharp pain shot up his arm, and he hollered out.

Brad came downstairs, followed by Selma. Selma had grabbed the small derringer gun hidden under her mattress on their way downstairs and hid it under her bra. When Brad went into the living room, he saw that no one was there.

"What the hell?" he exclaimed. He turned around to look

into the kitchen. He then felt a gun pressed to the back of his neck.

"Walk over to the basement," Selma told him.

She shoved Brad as he reached the opened door of the basement. Brad tumbled down into the basement and saw Keith strapped to a chair. He heard a loud bang from behind him and felt heat blossom on his left leg, followed by a sharp pain. Carter took a sledgehammer and let it fall on Brad's leg, right where Selma had just shot him. Taylor grabbed his arm and handcuffed him to a pipe.

When Tom walked out of the house with Andrew, he held his gun pressed to Andrew's back. They walked out of the fence gate of Andrew's front yard. Tom noticed a van parked by the curb that he hadn't seen before while staking out the Holbrooks' house. It was dark inside and seemed to be abandoned. But as he walked by, the sliding door opened, and a man quickly jumped out to grab him. As Tom turned to the man jumping at him, Andrew spun and elbowed Tom in the face. Both men pulled Tom into the van.

The man from the van immediately taped Tom's mouth shut with duct tape while Andrew used it to strap his hands behind his back like makeshift handcuffs. Tom looked closer at the man from the van and realized he seemed very familiar. This guy had started working at his factory not long before it shut down, or at least he started showing up around that time. In fact, he was the one who mentioned the robberies in wealthy neighbourhoods. He even pointed out the Holbrooks as potential targets to Tom, saying they would be easy to rob since they had no security. He was the one that inspired Tom to look into his illegal get-rich-quick scheme.

The man, whose name Andrew now remembered as being Kevin, taped his legs together.

"The factory has been closed for three months. I was wondering if your house was ever going to get hit," Kevin told Andrew.

Andrew started beating Tom and pistol-whipping him in the head. Tom pretended to be knocked out so he would stop. Andrew fell for the ploy.

"Someone finally did it. I'm glad you were able to make it to the party," Andrew said.

Tom learned from their conversation that they had planned everything. They had wanted to attract home invaders into their house so they could have their way with them. Meaning they lured people to invade their home so they could torture them. Tom realized they were truly sadistic people from the way they talked.

They traveled around communities with economic difficulties and used their connections and Kevin's expertise as an economist to destabilize them further. Then they identified who would be hit by it first and hit the hardest. Then Kevin would plant seeds, encouraging people to try and rob the Holbrooks. The Holbrooks had strategies to take the thieves captive instead. Once they were done having their fun with the thieves, they sent them off to prison. Afterwards, the Holbrooks would move away to a new town, saying that their current neighbourhood was just "too dangerous."

When Tom, Keith, and Brad had first walked into the living room and stepped on the wire embedded in the carpet, they set off a silent alarm. The wire was cut in ways that would only complete a circuit when stepped on in specific areas around the house. The circuit then lit up lights in the master bedroom and the kid's bedroom, warning them to prepare. Andrew had immediately texted Kevin, who was

Andrew's brother, to come and watch them in front of the house in case they needed a hand. They had cameras everywhere in the house except the bedrooms and basement. They used the footage to make it all look like self-defence.

Andrew got a text on his phone from Taylor. They were ready for him to come back into the house. He and Kevin dragged Tom to the basement door that led outside. They brought him in and threw him on the floor. Andrew kneeled down beside him, grinning down at him with a sinister look.

"I am going to break your fingers," he said with a smile.

He grabbed Tom's fingers and bent back the top joints as far as he could. Tom heard them crack, and the excruciating pain made him tear up. He tried to scream, but he could just make a muffled noise with the duct tape covering his mouth. Kevin got out some pliers and ripped out Tom's top front teeth.

"Hehehe. Look at him squirm," Kevin said mockingly.

Andrew and Taylor laughed along with them. Selma and Carter watched without any expression on their faces, not laughter, not disgust, not horror, nor any sympathy, absolutely nothing.

The family went on tormenting their captives for about thirty more minutes. They mocked and humiliated them, elicited pain, caused bruises, and made them bleed. They then contacted the police.

When the police arrived, Kevin had already left. The family told police how the men came in and invaded their home. Carter was able to escape and help his mother get to the basement, where they had tools that they could use to defend themselves. They talked about Keith getting the upper hand and threatening to kill them. They were extremely scared and did everything they could to protect themselves.

Andrew said he tricked Tom when they left the house by

saying he had left his card in the basement after working on a project the night before. He was thinking along the same lines to find something down there to protect himself with. Desperate, he grabbed a hammer to hit Tom in the face, but Tom blocked with his hand. This was how his fingers broke. When Andrew swung again, he broke some of Tom's teeth out.

Selma said that Brad had forced himself on her. When he was finally done with her, she grabbed the derringer she kept for protection and waited for the perfect opportunity. She saw her mother and brother had escaped and that the basement door was open. She decided to threaten Brad with the gun and took him to the basement to keep an eye on him and ensure her brother and mother were okay. On the way down, Brad turned to pull her, and she accidentally shot him in the leg.

The family showed the police video footage that corroborated their stories. The police were familiar with Brad; he had been in and out of jail a few times for drug-related charges. They saw the video from Selma's laptop and charged him with rape. Keith, Tom, and Brad were all charged with assault charges. They all got a lot more time than they would have for just the robbery. They tried to tell the judge what really happened. Tom told them everything he had overheard between Andrew and Kevin.

The judge thought the story sounded crazy. Using Occam's razor and feeling the videos and injuries fit the Holbrooks' story, the judge decided the Holbrooks were the ones telling the truth. Besides, Andrew and Taylor were well-to-do and respected members of society with clean records. Brad had a criminal record, and he, Keith, and Tom were in desperate situations. So, the original story made more sense.

The Holbrooks refused any interviews with the media. Andrew used his money and influence to keep mention of the incident to a minimum. After a few months, the Holbrooks moved to a different town in another state. They said they didn't feel safe in the neighbourhood they lived in now. That was the last time anyone in the town of Anderson ever saw them.

TROLL

"If you want to stop being afraid of something, you must invite it."

That is what one of Jane's boyfriends had told Ken.

"If you are scared of something, you have to make yourself go to the opposite of that emotion. You have to see the positive in what you are afraid of or turn the fear into something positive you can get excited about. That is how you don't let it control you. You become its friend and invite it."

Ken thought about these words as his bedtime rolled around. It was 9:00 p.m. on a school night. He would rather sleep in the living room or not at all. But at 11 years old, he did not have much of a choice in the matter.

Ken's room was underneath the stairs. It was strange, he had never seen a house with a room underneath the stairs until they moved here about a month ago. Ken had thought the room was cool. It was like a secret hiding place. The ceiling inside was shaped at an angle to allow the stairs to fit where they were. Since staying in it, he did not find the room so exciting anymore. In fact, he hated it.

The last couple of nights, in the corner of his room, right underneath the stairs, he could feel someone watching him. It was extra dark in that space when the lights were out. He would sleep in his room with the light on, but his mother's current boyfriend would not allow it. Josh, Jane's latest love affair, said that Ken needed to stop being a scared little boy and learn to sleep with the light off. That was the only way Ken would learn there was nothing going bump in the night.

Every night at bedtime, Josh would come to make sure Ken had his lights off. Jane backed Josh up on this. Ken was tempted to turn the light on after he was in bed. But he was too afraid to do so. The switch was right beside that dark corner underneath the stairs. He imagined something might reach out to grab him if he went to turn on the light.

Jane was used to Ken being scared. He was scared of a lot of things. He was scared of any living thing that wasn't a dog or a cat or a human. He was scared of the bullies who picked on him at his previous school. Luckily, he transferred schools when they moved into this house. The bullies used to knock books out of his hands and try to intimidate him. They always tripped him while he was walking down the hallways. They humiliated him at every chance they got.

Jane's former boyfriend, Kyle, told him to invite what he was afraid of. He taught him a few moves to use on the bullies. If he had fought the bullies, he might have been one step closer to conquering his fears. Instead, Ken just tried to avoid them.

He did like Kyle though. He was always nice to him and told him interesting things. Kyle had his own ideas about the Bible that he would teach Ken, especially about Adam and Eve. He said what changed in Adam and Eve was self-awareness. They had become conscious. According to him, that is why Adam and Eve had felt shame. They covered their nakedness and tried to lie about what they did.

The serpent had actually helped them to obtain the gift of consciousness for themselves. This is how they acquired knowledge of good and evil, or at least the ability to discern between the two. He said that good and evil are based on suffering. Things that make one suffer are learned to be evil, whereas things that lead to relief and joy are good. Before the Tree of Knowledge, Adam and Eve could not know this because they were not truly aware or reflective enough to grasp the concepts of suffering and joy. This is why they suffered after they ate from the tree. It was part of the mixed bag of gifts and curses that came with self-awareness. Humans had to go from no self-awareness to self-awareness at some point in their evolutionary history, which is what that story represents.

Kyle was full of unique ideas like this. Ken found them interesting and entertaining. He was upset when Kyle and his mom broke up. He missed him a lot. But despite Kyle's efforts at helping him overcome his fear, Ken was still unable to do so. He was still scared of the dark. He had always been afraid of the dark.

But tonight was different. Not only did he feel like something else was in the room with him. The last few nights, he had heard a low, rolling growl from that dark corner underneath the stairs. It wasn't a very loud growl. But it was a prolonged, menacing growl. It always sounded like it was building up to a roar, which it never did. It was hardly the type of thing he could just invite to him. He didn't want to invite this frightening thing to have dinner with him or play with him. He was too afraid to do that.

When he told his mom and Josh about it the next day, they were unsympathetic. That evening, he turned out the light again and jumped into bed. He stared into the dark corner underneath the stairs and started hearing the same growl he had heard on previous nights. As he looked in the corner, his eyes adjusted a little. He definitely saw something with dark, scraggly hair sticking out of the top of its head. It looked like it was crouching down. As with previous nights, Ken did not sleep well at all that night.

When he arrived at his new school the next morning, he looked tired. One of the other kids asked him if he was sleepy, to which he just nodded his head. The other kid, Patrick, started asking him questions, as some children do to a new face.

"Where do you live?" Patrick asked Ken.

"I live on Pearce Street. The big house with the woods and creek to the back," Ken responded.

"I know the place. That is where a kid who lived there a few years ago went missing. One night, she went to bed, and nobody ever saw her again. There was no sign of anyone breaking in, so the police investigated the parents. There was never enough evidence to convict them, but the town was divided on whether they had killed her or not. Those who knew the parents knew how devastated they were and how much they loved their daughter. Others were not so convinced. They finally moved away, unable to deal with all the judgemental stares and hate mail they received," Patrick said.

"I wonder if they did it. Maybe they got away with it," Ken said, somewhat out of curiosity but mostly to keep the conversation going.

"What is weird is that a couple of kids have gone missing or died in that area. One kid wandered into the woods behind that house. He went missing for several days before the police found his body in those woods by the creek. It was torn up. The police said a wild animal, probably a bear, got a hold of him. A bear was spotted wandering around at the same time, and animal control had to take care of it. But a lot of folks said a bear wouldn't do the damage that was done to that kid. His parents were devastated."

"There was one other. This was last summer. A girl. She was older, maybe sixteen, I think. Her body was found on the train tracks that go through the woods behind your house. It was ruled a suicide. Authorities said she dove in front of the train, right beside where it goes over the bridge. I think it is a weird way to commit suicide. Other townsfolk agree that it was weird too, but that is the official report of the investigation."

"You seem to know a lot about these deaths and disappearances, especially for someone your age," Ken said somewhat suspiciously.

"I knew the kid who lived in the house. The one that went missing. Her name was Heather. Her parents adored her. She told me that she was scared to sleep in her room. Of course, her parents made her. She was not the type to get scared or believe in anything weird. But she said something watched her in the dark in her room underneath the stairs. She was sure some creature lived under there and hid in the dark. In fact, she thought it was only visible in the dark. She said she saw it once when she shined a flashlight at it. It was only a glance, but she described it as an ugly man-beast of some kind. It looked strong, with sharp claws and teeth and random patches of fur on its body. The rest of its body looked like dry skin. I don't know how she saw all that so quickly, but she swore on it. She said it had seemed surprised when she shined the flashlight on it. It covered its face and tried to move away from the flashlight's beam. Then it vanished. She looked all over and saw nothing. She wasn't the type to make up wild stories. Two days after she told me about this, she vanished."

After hearing Patrick's stories, Ken was sure he would not make up for much sleep that night either. But he was really tired and struggled to stay awake, so he fell asleep early on the couch while watching television. He hoped his mom and Josh would leave him there, but they made him get up and go to bed.

Before he went to bed, he went to the bathroom beside his mother's room. Josh kept his camping stuff in one of the bedroom closets. Ken remembered there was a battery-powered lantern among his stuff. While his mother and Josh were still in the living room, he snuck into their bedroom and looked through the closet. He found the lantern underneath Josh's tent. He took it and went straight to his room so they would not see he had it.

He decided he would switch the lantern on after Josh came to check that his bedroom light was off. But Ken was so exhausted he fell asleep before Josh checked on him, and he did not wake after Josh opened the door to look. Ken woke up to the sound of a low, gurgling growl that did not sound like any animal he knew of.

As he woke and got his bearings, he realized the sound was coming from right beside his bed. He looked and saw some sort of creature crouched beside him. Its breath was hot on his skin. He felt a claw slowly moving up the blanket toward his face. He felt the lamp beside his left hand underneath the blanket. He slowly reached for it so as not to let the creature know he was up to anything. Then, as quickly as he could, he flicked the switch and threw off the blanket, shining the light everywhere around him.

As he did this, the creature raced back to the corner and disappeared into it, right in front of Ken's eyes. The creature's skin had looked rough and tough. Other than that, the skins seemed almost human, but the patches of fur seemed animal-like. The creature had looked so startled when Ken turned the light on. In that moment, he saw drool dripping from its sharp teeth as it loomed over Ken.

He left the lamp on for the rest of that night and slept well that night.

The next day at school, Ken saw Patrick and told him what had happened.

"You are lucky I told you about it, Ken. You could have been another missing kid this morning or even a dead one."

"After our conversation yesterday, I found a book in my dad's study. He collects books on local history and legends," Patrick said, pulling out a book. The title read, "Strange Happenings in Fairplay County."

"There is a chapter here about a man from the early 1900s who talks about a creature living in our town. He even mentions the woods where all the strange stories I told you about happened. He calls it a troll and figures it travels through invisible passageways or tunnels. He theorizes these tunnels may exist in a different dimension. The gateways to these tunnels are invisible and can only be used by the troll," Patrick told him.

"Apparently, people had disappeared periodically in this area. It is like the troll rests for several years before becoming active again. When this town was first settled, people talked about some beast in the woods. Young people, mainly kids, would disappear or die under mysterious circumstances. Some believed it was a pack of wolves or a bear. But nobody had ever seen a creature that would do the things that this one did to people. People were ripped apart. Their limbs were found scattered about. Eventually, it stopped as suddenly as it started, and nobody saw any signs of the creature again. They assumed whatever it was had moved on or died."

"When this man moved to town, the disappearances had started again. One person saw the creature while hiking through the woods one night. It was feasting on a child's dead body. The person kept quiet and managed to get back home. There is a sketch right here of what he saw."

Patrick pointed at the picture. Ken looked at it. It was creepy and gave him goosebumps all over. The creature looked exactly like what he had seen last night. He told Patrick this.

"See, there is something to this. He said it was a troll, and for some reason, the gates to its invisible tunnels were under bridges and stairs. Exactly where trolls were believed to have lived in ancient times. He says trolls were sometimes called house spirits, but he doesn't think they actually lived in houses. The houses were just structured in certain ways near a troll's home that gave it access." Patrick explained.

"He also said that Trolls appeared in caves, and he actually believed this troll lived in a specific cave. You can see where he marked it on this map right here." Patrick pointed at a sketched-out map in the book. "I know this cave. I have seen it. It's almost at the centre of where all these weird things have been happening. It is not far from your house. I think this is where we can get rid of the troll. We may be able to find Heather there too."

Ken's eyes grew wide as he realized where Patrick was going with this. "You want us to sneak into a deep, dark cave to kill this thing? How? We don't know if it can be killed. And I hate to tell you this, but this thing kills. I am sure Heather is dead."

Patrick shrugged his shoulders. "Maybe, but it does rest for years at a time. Maybe some of the disappearances are kids it keeps to eat during this rest period. Maybe it is like a hibernation period where it stores food for itself. And I know it is scary. I have not seen this thing in real life as you have. I understand if you do not want to tag along. But this may be the only way to save your life too. It almost got you last night. I don't know how many more nights you may have before you become another victim."

Ken looked down in thought. "Okay, but how are we going to kill this thing? Put a permanent light source in the cave?"

"Maybe then we can corner it by shining lights at the other gates at the same time. That seems like a sound idea," Patrick said.

Ken said, "But couldn't it just hide in these invisible tunnels until the light goes out?"

"I am not sure if these tunnels are actual places or if they are just shortcuts to each gate that are all connected directly to the cave. We need to do this during the day so there is light everywhere. I think it is worth a shot," Patrick answered.

Ken let out a huge sigh as if he already regretted agreeing to go on this venture.

"Okay, maybe we should get more of those battery-powered lamps. How many do you think we need?" Ken asked.

"I am not sure exactly. We need to get as many as we possibly can. I am not sure how big that cave is. We also need to keep the light on in your room. We need one for the bridge the railroad goes over. I know of a tree with a small hole in the bottom of it I suspect is a gate. It is near where the boy was 'killed by an animal'," Patrick said, pantomiming quotation gestures in the air with his fingers. "I got some allowance saved up. There should be a few hundred dollars. We can use it to buy the lamps," Patrick continued.

After school, they bought out all the battery-powered lamps from a hardware and camping store. They also bought enough batteries for each. They decided to light up the gates they knew of first. They kept Ken's bedroom light on. They put a lamp under the bridge to chase away any shadows. Another lamp went underneath the tree that Patrick suspected of being a gate. Then they set off for the cave.

They stood at the mouth of the cave, trying to control their fear. Patrick carried a baseball bat with a long nail hammered through the top. They both carried backpacks with the lanterns in them. Ken had a lot of fear to suppress. He was already scared of the dark. He was certainly scared of murderous trolls. Dark caves didn't seem too inviting either.

He remembered what Kyle had told him. Invite what you are afraid of. It was like Patrick and him were on an adventure, just like in fantasy books and RPG games. They were adventurers and soon-to-be heroes, he thought. Although a thought in the back of his mind said, *or soon to be dead*.

The entrance to the cave was small. Ken and Patrick had to crawl through. Thankfully, they were able to stand just a few feet inside. It was very dark. Without the lanterns, they could not see their hands in front of their faces. They continued deeper into the cave with Ken's lantern lighting their path. The cave system went underground and was much bigger than it looked from the outside.

After journeying inward for a while, Ken thought he heard something scuffling in a corner. He shined his lantern to where he had heard the noise but didn't see anything. He figured it may have been his imagination. At least, he hoped that was all it was.

The Lantern began to flicker, and he gasped as went out. He tried to turn the switch off and then back on. It did nothing. He heard a scuffling noise coming at him fast. He was terrified. For a moment, the thought crossed his mind that this may be his last moment alive. Suddenly a light shined behind him. The creature quickly scurried back into the dark. He heard a growl just beyond the light's limit.

Patrick had pulled out a lantern from Ken's backpack and

turned it on. He got a glance at the creature just before it ran back into the dark.

"That is one ugly-looking beast," he said. "Is that the lantern you got from home? Did you change the batteries?" Patrick asked.

"N-n-no," Ken stammered.

"Well, put some new batteries in it. Let's start laying these things out," Patrick told him.

They placed the lanterns from the entrance to where they were now. They had more than enough to ensure there were no shadows behind any rocks. They looked in every corner and every crack, but they found nothing.

There was no sign of the troll. There were bones in the cave. Some of the bones looked old. Some looked not so old. Then in a depression in the back of the cave, Ken saw a young girl. There was a chain around her wrist attached to the cave wall. She was covered in scars and blood-stained clothes. Her hair looked scraggly.

"Heather!" Patrick cried out.

"Patrick?" the girl quietly asked the mysterious voice that had called her name. He ran to her and tried to get the chain off. He hit it with his bat. But all of his efforts were in vain.

"We need to go get help," Patrick said.

"Please don't leave me," Heather pleaded.

"We have the lanterns all over the cave. The thing can't exist in light. You will be safe," Patrick told her.

"Please…" she pleaded again.

Patrick looked at her and saw the terror and sadness in her eyes.

"You stay here, and I can go get help from my mom and her boyfriend. My house isn't far," Ken told Patrick.

Patrick nodded his head in agreement. Ken took the rest of the lanterns with him. He climbed out of the cave, which relieved him, although he felt guilty since Patrick and

ON THE BORDERS OF REALITY

Heather were still in there. He ran towards his house, looking for anything else that could be potential gates for the troll. He looked for deep dark holes, bridges, and caves. He did find a rock formation with a depression underneath a rock ledge. He threw a switched-on lantern into it. He didn't see a sign of anything having been there. But he figured you could never be too safe.

He reached home and ran inside. "Mom! Josh!" he yelled.

"What?" Josh yelled from their bedroom. Ken had no doubt they were doing things he didn't like to imagine his mother doing.

"Somebody needs help!" Ken yelled.

"What? Hold on!" Josh yelled back.

He heard messing around coming from their room upstairs. He then heard a noise coming from his room. He looked over at it. It sounded like something was scuffling around in there. He looked at the crack at the bottom of the door and saw the light was off. The room had no windows, so it was pitch dark in there, even during the daytime.

He went to the bedroom door and opened it. He didn't go in. He saw the creature's outline standing in the middle of his room. It looked like it was ready to pounce. He was too scared to reach in there and turn the light switch on.

Ken found his mom's cell phone on the living room table. He grabbed it, turned the flashlight app on, and then shined it at the creature. It moved out of the way of the light, closer to the light switch. He hoped it would move away so he could turn on the light switch. He was close to the door. A gray hand with long fingers and long claws shot from the darkness and pulled him into the room.

Ken waved the phone's flashlight around his room, trying to hit the creature with it. The creature managed to avoid it, and he dropped the phone. The creature lifted him up. While suspended in the air, Ken's foot grazed against the wall where the light switch was. He turned the switch on with his foot. The beast let out a high-pitched blood-curdling scream. It went wild around the room, running into things and breaking stuff.

Ken's mom and Josh ran to the doorway.

"What the fuck?" Josh yelled. Then the beast suddenly burst into flames and burned away. There was no trace left of its body—just some scorch marks on the floor where it burned.

"What the hell was that?" Jane asked.

"We've been calling it a troll," Ken said.

"What?" Jane asked, confused.

"I found the missing girl. She is chained up in a cave in the woods. I can't get the chain off," Ken said.

"What? What have you been doing?" Josh asked. "Never mind. I have some bolt cutters in the closet with my other tools."

Josh grabbed them and followed Ken to the cave. It was too tight of a fit for Josh. So, he let Ken go into the cave with the bolt cutters while Jane called the police.

Ken got back to Heather and Patrick and cut the chain. They all got out of the cave as fast as they could. There were police waiting for them outside when they exited the cave.

Heather hugged Patrick and Ken and said, "Thank you."

The police took her to the hospital for a medical and mental evaluation. She did end up needing some medical treatment, but she recovered well. The police contacted Heather's parents, who drove all night and half a day to get to her as fast as possible. They hugged her while tears ran down their faces.

Ken, Patrick, and Heather told their stories. They told their parents and the authorities about the creature. It was decided that some maniac did this to Heather, and it was so scary that the children remembered him as a monster. The evaluators said their minds were suppressing the truth of what had happened, and they remembered the man as a fairy tale creature to make it easier for them to cope.

Ken wasn't sure how this was easier to cope with. He told Josh and his mom to tell them that they saw the creature burning. They refused. They said they were unsure what they saw, but they knew no one would believe them and didn't want to face ridicule. Worse, they could be accused of fueling the children's delusions.

Fairplay County police continued to look for a psychopath that they never found. Nor did the psychopath ever strike again. They figured he had moved on or was trying to lay low. But no mysterious deaths or missing people ever happened in Fairplay County again.

WHERE'S THE TRUTH?

They say the truth is out there
Some say it's in us
Either way, it don't seem fair
No matter how I search and fuss
I can't find it anywhere
I've prayed to different gods
But they all stay quiet
Tried to sell my soul to the devil
He won't buy it
I've read the messages from God
Listened to men of science
Explored ideas that are odd
But they all seem blinded
From where we're from and where we go
There seems no satisfactory answer
Delusion new and old
They spread like cancer
Truth from revelation, observation, or reason
None seem worthy of total reliance
To do that to truth seems like treason

Whether philosophy, religion, or science
Are we mortal or infinite
Is there something hidden or what we see we get?
Maybe I should be happy being here, this minute
Be grateful and live it
I'm not trying to get glory
There is no need
But maybe hidden in a story
There's a seed…

ABOUT THE AUTHOR

Timothy Foreman lives in Oconee, South Carolina. There he enjoys the mountains and reading. He lives with his wife, Amanda, and their daughter, Anastasia. He works as a psych nurse. He has been studying and striving to understand the overlap between science and the paranormal since he was a teenager. This has brought him down a variety of paths in search of truth and knowledge.

Printed in the USA
CPSIA information can be obtained
at www.ICGtesting.com
LVHW042047021223
765141LV00057B/921

9 781088 137352